Steal Stuff From Work

Jasper Pierce

SPINELESS BOOKS  URBANA, ILLINOIS

This one is for the ones the other ones weren't for.

Even in Seattle the drought goes on. *The late summer skies test our endurance as we stagger with thirst beneath unreachable rainclouds. All our moisture, it seems, is reclaimed by the insidious air. In late fees and reconnections, in parking tickets and auto repairs, in hospital and funeral bills, every silver drop spent, spilt, trickles back into the sky.*

We work all day to drink all night. Tossed by alcoholic nightmares, we soak our sheets. In the morning, not even a stain remains.

It was the busiest night of the year. Friday night, graduation weekend at the University of Washington. One cook and two waiters had called in sick. From the back of the kitchen, I saw the extant waitstaff come in from the front dining room looking white, glazed with fear, with twice their normal number of tables refilling themselves unstoppably, customers lined up out the door, having waited for an hour to be seated, each party a family dressed tastefully and obviously forcing a celebratory air. You would take their drink orders and come upon them again ten minutes and fifteen tables later struggling to remember them as they looked up with imploring eyes. They recognized you, they knew your name, you were their only chance at surviving this restaurant with celebratory air still intact. But you had no idea who they were despite having previously engaged them in hypnotized small talk during which you guessed who had graduated and congratulated them and asked their major while your mind crawled with appetizers, checks, remembered forgotten errands such as Dijon mustard or a peppermill or even a cocktail napkin a particular and labor-intensive customer might have requested for a spilled drop of martini or perhaps just to test you, to prove that you really were willing to jump through the smallest imaginable hoop even in the stormiest of weather on this special special night.

Where were their orders?

The waitstaff would come into the kitchen looking white, transmitting the tension of angry customers toward certain imperative unbegun steaks, salmon, or veal medallions. The overworked cooks glared back with paring knives in their eyes.

The waitstaff would come in looking white, except, that is, for Cy. Cy gleamed like a messiah, and all you saw in his eyes was cash. Short, stocky, with big glasses, an owl in a tuxedo shirt, he played the kitchen staff like a piano. He was a pro, issuing staccato orders, reminders, retractions — irritating in his punctiliousness but refreshing in his unaffected, audible brevity — an expert air traffic controller in a thunderstorm. And oh yes his orders would all come through perfect and on time and with only minimal injuries perpetrated by enraged cooks — the filet that had fallen on the floor served up as pretty as a photo on the cover of *Restaurant* magazine, or garlic alfredo infected with invisible traces of saliva, mucus, pus, blood, semen, or who knows what revolting bodily fluid. Or Cy would inform the cooks who the richest pricks in the crowd were and the cooks might experiment with the dinners, work out their vengeance that way. And by the end of the night when the crew had regrouped barside, Cy would buy, a puffing suspendered bow-tied penguin emperor, in a blur of generosity dispensing upon the cooks less than they were worth but more than they had ever been given.

And if Cy had broken $500 in tips, admitting to perhaps $150 of it for tax purposes, this currency converted to charisma, and then maybe even I, Sir Kemp the dishwasher, might be invited to join in a round of shots underwritten by Cy, who also overtipped his bartender, keeping vital the gratuity economy on which he was financially and emotionally dependent. And, believe me, he didn't have to buy me a shot. Working the cooks to get his orders served up unerringly and swiftly was how he brought down his cash. But in the end, where I worked, it didn't matter to the customers how well or quickly I washed their plates. Cy rode the cooks for the dishes, the cooks rode me for clean plates, I rode the bussers for the dirty plates, and I might ever interact with Cy only if I waited too long to run a rack of water glasses through the machine and then he would be in my face for the moment. But I was not anxious to get attention. I worked like a wench, truth be told, and became the star dishwasher for nights like these. Shifts like these, obviously, were not popular among dishwashers. Only for the waiters and the owner did a crescendo of commerce bring a corresponding surge in wage.

But I could get away with a lot, and, if I turned the dishes around, and if, when they saw me working, they saw me working like a wench, and if I kept the servers in water glasses still so hot from the dishwasher they might crack if you poured ice in them, and if I kept at least two saucepans of every size hanging where the cooks could grab them without looking, and if I unloaded the bustubs so the bussers might grab them back, then, even if I made use of every horizontal surface to stack procrastinated saucers, tupperware, parfait glasses, baking sheets, they left me alone with the whole back of the restaurant and its storage areas at my disposal, with me knowing that by the end of the night — a night like this might finally end by two a.m. if the closers didn't drink too much (but they would) — when the floor was mopped, the register drawer in the safe, and half the inventory gone, nobody would be in any kind of condition to count how many steaks and how many swordfish. The math would work itself backward, reverse-engineering the expected totals. Yes, in a buzz of activity nobody would notice anything I did, and if I moved fast enough to keep abreast of the buzz, if I truly worked like only a wench would work, well, I might just extend to myself the exemplary and generous customer service the restaurant as a matter of policy offered, and similarly extend the concept of gratuities to myself, and extend the concept of working on commission to myself. I might go home with any number of tips, bonuses, or incentives: rewards for a job well done.

Distraction is key to prestidigitation. Don't avoid attention, control it. I whistled while I worked.

My earliest memories are of my grandmother's farmhouse in Iowa. Three floors of treasure. A coin collection, a gilded porcelain chamber pot, a wooden trunk of photo albums and ancient newspaper clippings, a feather bed and, in a red canister filled with generations of toys, a children's book called *Gillespie and the Guards*. Since my last name was Gillespie, I took the book for an heirloom, some important family document.

The Gillespie in the book was a peasant kid in feudal times. He got a temp job in the King's castle. Every day he would be seen leaving work pushing a wheelbarrow filled with something worthless. Straw, sand, gravel. At the palace gate, the guards always searched the contents of the wheelbarrow to make sure Gillespie wasn't trying to rip off the King but they never found anything.

Turns out Gillespie was stealing wheelbarrows.

I used to wonder what Gillespie wanted with all those wheelbarrows.

But now I understand.

The food and kitchen supplies I took were no better than wheelbarrows. There was no way to get money for them that I knew of. But stealing them was a game I could not quit.

I only ever wanted to be a writer. I've had jobs every day of my life since I was eight. My spirit had just about been hammered flat. Working took its toll on me, until the day I started taking my toll on it. I had become so exhausted and demoralized that by the end of the day I was no longer taking any of myself home from work. So I started taking some of my work home with me.

I guess I'm something of a criminal.

I steal stuff from work.

I've never been caught, and always moved from one job to the next with a good reference. And I'm principled. I never steal from coworkers or customers, only from the job itself. My patterns outwit inventory, my operations on the edges of what is known or plausible.

I am committed to breaking even.

And understand that I'm not the only one.

The rush had passed. While most of the restaurant's work was ending, mine was just beginning. The evening's flashflood of business was draining into my area, floating stacks of bustubs from the dining room and pots and pans from the kitchen, the dreaded clam chowder tureen with its rubbery, unscrubbable inner skin. The seven-foot cook Iain ducked out from under the ventilator hood, threw his apron in the laundry bag, and headed back to the break area, an unlit cigarette already in his fingers. The cooks were a fun bunch of miscreants. Two of them lived in prison, contracted to the restaurant every evening for two dollars an hour, half of which was claimed by their work-release program. Derek the chef impressed his crew by rolling up the white sleeve of his double-breasted chef's uniform and immersing his entire hand in steaming lobster bisque, demonstrating no pain. In the eyes of the cooks this mettle impressed any skeptics who may have doubted he was managerial material, and his disregard for the most basic protocols of hygiene only reinforced their respect. Drunks, prisoners, illegals and me. Today's game involved playing catch with knives. Cy paused to admire their antics.

"Seattle Globetrotters. Take it on the road, make some real money."

"Cyrus, catch!" Derek faked tossing a cleaver. Cy blinked but did not flinch. He moved on, barely smiling.

"Somebody oughta chop that boy a new mouth."

"Slice and dice."

"Serve him up. Pan-sear him."

"Asshole sauté."

"Fried leech."

"Throw a little garlic butter and capers on there, get rid of that sour monkey taste."

I heard the tinkle of ice: the chef had just been delivered his *aperitif*; the owner had left the building. The kitchen radio abruptly increased in volume, echoing through the metal racks of canned goods, the soup warmers, the burners. Derek asked me to grab him a steak from the walk-in cooler. Past the thick metal door and into the frosty enclosure where billows of refrigerated air swirled between shelves of perishables, I selected one steak for Derek and another for my breakfast. Outside the walk-in door, between the block tables used for prep work, in the big kitchen garbage can on wheels, were not one but two garbage bags, the second hidden beneath the first, twisted closed. It would have looked as though I were throwing something away but nobody looked. I delivered the meat to the kitchen and took out the trash – one bag for the dumpster, one filled with frozen meat and a bottle of sherry for my refrigerator. Garbage is a great hiding place.

With that, it was time to take my break, the abrupt supper before the real work began. Ordinarily I might have my choice of entrees prepared by a sympathetic cook. I was the best dishwasher, and even though I was a bit of a college boy they fed me well and I let them know I appreciated their work. But tonight I might as well ask one of the survivors of the Titanic to swim down and fetch my keys from the bottom of the pool as ask one of the cooks to cook for me. Pushed to the side of the shiny metal kitchen window was a ghetto of five-star entrees, twenty- to thirty-dollar dishes sent back by customers or ordered incorrectly by dazed and flustered waitstaff. Some of them had been under the heatlamps for awhile, plates too hot to touch, and perhaps Cy had absently shoveled half of one in his mouth with one hand while with the other he flipped through his tickets, remaining on top of the game, his mind culling the first five things to do and assimilating them into one long and complicated action he would then execute with an unhurried but insistent precision. He wasn't the most handsome waiter nor the tallest, but the handsome and tall ones might end up giving him any number of their overloaded tables, opting under duress for the less profitable path.

I selected an abandoned chicken saltimbocca, apparently unmolested albeit somewhat congealed. In the breakroom there was nothing to steal but an ashtray. I would never have done that. At this point in the evening it was a very popular ashtray, an attractive spa resort to the sweaty and disheveled angels of service. Asking the five or six of them not to smoke while I ate might have produced some mild comic effect, but more likely the assertion would have gone evidently unnoticed and be passed back to me in an acrid rejoinder days or weeks later. Like me, they all had a lot of work yet to do, but the part of the arc where people might scream at each other had passed.

Everyone present had been deepfried in adrenalin and stress and had, with injuries, survived.

Each had survived, that is, except Cy. Cyrus had triumphed. In his blur he had in fact already finished his share of the closing tasks. Since he had been handed other servers' tables during the rush, now he handed back two-tops coming in for dessert drinks, small tabs, and long conversations. Cy paid back his fifties in fives. None of these customers would calculate their tip based on how many refills of coffee they had been offered nor how many hours they had stayed, and Cy, his eyes big behind his huge glasses, lit a cigarette, slipped on his trenchcoat, said he'd see us later, and walked, still smoking, through the kitchen and out the back exit.

"He left in a hurry," Jane remarked.

"You never count your money / when you're sitting at the table," sang an astute busboy.

"No shit. Know when to walk away and know when to run."

In a corner, Iain, rubbing a newly bandaged wrist, was on a cellphone gently cooing lies to his wife, telling her he would be home late, assuring her that he would not get drunk.

"Honey? Two beers. Just two beers."

All gave way to bitter laughter.

We pretended we had turned our backs on it, but the world had actually pulled away from us. *We had seen the blade between rich and poor and, in the fresh conscience of youth, couldn't side with the privileged, their bland lawns and weak, fake music. But we learned we weren't strong enough to suffer, and when we turned back to accept our station, the train had moved on. Some of us still held toys we grew up with: superheroes, soldiers, spacemen and beautyqueens in shoeboxes. They reminded us of a time when we thought we could decide what we would become. But that world had submerged to a hazy sediment of sentiment. We were embarrassed to recall how our families took vacations, bought furniture, made decisions, were rewarded for work with leisure. That sharp paradox of childhood we tried to blunt with drugs and alcohol. Now even water bills were too much for us — never mind owning homes, redecorating, landscaping or upgrading to a better car. What was wrong with us that we couldn't pay for childcare, tuition or a trip to the dentist? Given every chance to become middle class, we had fallen flat. When we were infants, parents had grabbed our tiny hands, pulled us to our feet, got us walking, outfitted us with shoes and braces, allotted us allowance, nourished us with four food groups, television and biannual gifts, and sent us toddling out the door where we fell in the mud and came knocking to ask for our rooms back. They had given us a better education than they had, better health care, better nutrition. The advanced science of childrearing and early childhood education had been applied to our cause. We had multivitamins, aerobic exercise, educational television, summer school, Sunday school, after-school specials, Playskool toys, school lunches, Schoolhouse Rock and stereo, and yet we couldn't get a career. Were we soft? Did we lack integrity? Was it necessary to have been born into a Cold War world of corporal punishment, unsafe playground equipment and dirt clods in order to have the grit to succeed? We took fast-food jobs at age sixteen and settled in. Stalled on the first rung, we majored in humanities, received the best classical education and burned out in cheap rented rooms. We convinced ourselves we were rebelling against conformity, consumerism, sobriety, but we started to suspect we couldn't handle what our parents did. Our grandfathers hated us. They were old men—withered, weathered, liver-spotted, raised on DDT, lard and tobacco. They had zero curiosity or tolerance, considered open-mindedness tantamount to indiscipline and were deaf to music. They hobbled across their perfect lawns with an arsenal of herbicidal poisons and loud gasoline-burning power tools, eradicating every last tree or dubious plant. We were supposed to be taking care of them by this stage in the game, but we had* *refused to relinquish our roles as children, did not mature like stocks, bonds and Roth IRAs. When, at age fourteen, we had dyed our hair blue, they had words with us. When, at age thirty, we dyed our hair blue, they were careful not to express anything, for fear of giving us something further to rebel against. We were a bad investment; they swallowed their loss. They blamed themselves for their failure, sensing correctly that to blame us for ours would wreck us further. We started to believe them—we were losers, they were winners. But it wasn't us. They had staked their claim on a high watermark, riding the roller coaster of American prosperity over the parabola of the millennium before the slow, accelerating fall. The landscape had changed so gradually that nobody had noticed the tilt.*

Flogged, I came home to nobody. My jeans were soaked with dishwater from the knees down. I peeled them off, leaving them in a puddle on the kitchen floor. I smelled like fish. I pulled a sixpack from a paper bag, collapsed in a chair, propped my numb feet on an overturned wheelbarrow. The sixer sat atop three hardback volumes and did not live long enough to get warm. I unlatched the prison window high on my basement apartment wall. A breeze pushed in. Something thumped somewhere in the apartment. The air had a barely restrained violence. Clouds erased the sky. Grey buzzed in the silent auditorium of night. Crumpled pages lay across the table, broken notions. And then silence. Old machines with corroded bolts, I thought, ran themselves in an installation behind a rusted barbed wire fence deep in the country at the end of an uninviting road. No people go there, no cars parked there, just a clanking and smoke rising from a chimney. Another beer, gratuitous and abusive, and not enough of it. An abrupt and angry wind picked up a stinging cloud of dust. I stood, face to the window, and stared up and out. The people walking by on the sidewalk turned familiar. I knew their muted foggy glamour as they flashed through headlights beneath a pink neon cursive typographic affluence. Sunken men conducted tense relations with idling cars. My mind became a telephone and I called them up to tell them. A car alarm went off. I had been disconnected. I thought it might rain but it didn't. I lifted a glass to the sky. Still later I typed something but did not know what.

At three in the afternoon the alarm chiseled into my dream. I found myself inside a person sprawled on a couch, lint-mouthed. My bookmark had read a hundred pages and there was a poem in my notebook I did not recognize. And, as I stood bearded with shaving cream at my dry sink, the faucet silent, I looked deep into my eyes with searching honesty and understood the water had been shut off.

I went to work early and told the owner I wanted to move up to the floor, become a waiter.

He was uncomfortable with that. There was no concept of promotion in restauranteering; it was purely a caste system. My year of impeccable service as a dishwasher meant only that I was an indispensable dishwasher. Of course he didn't know that I hadn't paid for food, alcohol, kitchen utensils, light bulbs or coffee since the week I started.

His face was a bad cut of meat. But he saw that I meant it.

The previous night, inexplicably, a full tropical fishtank had disappeared from the dining room. For the moment, it looked like somebody might be fired. The owner was all too willing to add extra waitstaff on the spot. He hired me.

I left for a bowtie and tuxedo shirt, studs and a cummerbund, and overturned my apartment in search of any not-yet-empty bottle.

I returned to the wake of an execution. The kitchen staff had evacuated to the alley where they used cigarettes and appraised with song college girls passing on the street. Jane got the axe for the stolen fishtank. She left the restaurant shrieking curses with such abandon that all hearts were punctured — even the owner may have felt a twinge of something. A single mother who was thoroughly focused on the task of survival, that she had stolen a tropical fishtank as a prank was inconceivable. But she was not a hottie, was slow, had told off the owner at least once and memorably, so he fired her to set an example for the real culprit, and to settle the matter before golf.

It was all wrong. I had never waited tables before. In the kitchen we frowned on that sort of prostitution. I was only peripherally familiar with the menu. And it was still graduation weekend. Jane had been there a long time and knew the menu as well as anybody, certainly better than the younger waitresses. She was direct and sincere. Nobody believed she was responsible for the theft, and her dismissal enraged the other waitstaff, who resented my presence in the waitstation, spurning me before the ranks of dirty cola nozzles and blackened coffeepots. They acted as though I had been the one to fire her when in fact she had been one of the only servers who had ever spoken to me. They behaved as though they might force me out and reverse the tragedy. They were not going to help me my first night, and the only one who would deal with me—whether because he had a heart, or because a catastrophe in my section would make the entire evening go that much less smoothly for everyone—was Cy, who explained the basics. He was uninvolved in the restaurant's politics, would not miss Jane and was focused on the task at hand: Saturday night graduation rush. On the chalkboard by the kitchen window where the specials were listed we would write *85* when we were almost out and *86* when we were out. That was one of many details I could never have guessed.

Once Cy had caught me smoking a joint in the walk-in. I don't know what he was going in there for — it was off limits to floor staff. But he laughed and left, and this contact seemed to have brought us together on a level beneath the others.

Waistapron hanging before me like a loincloth, I rehearsed insincere endorsements of the specials to my first table, Mr. "Call-Me-Adam" White, an eccentric regular who ate alone, always there to request his usual table the moment we unlocked the front door. By the time he had talked me through his usual special order, three more families were seated in my section with open menus, looking around. Tom the manager glared at me as I went back to the kitchen. "I'll be right with you." "I'll be right with you." "I'll be right with you." From the outside of the metal kitchen window I clipped my ticket to the wheel and spun it so it faced the cooks. Derek took one look at the ticket, and spun it so it was facing me again. "No," he said. Cy appeared, grabbed my ticket, snapped three of his in its place, spun the wheel, pulled out a blank, and translated my longhand into the kitchen's preferred notation. If you wrote *sour cream* they would give you bad cream, if you wrote *scream* they would give you sour cream. Cy snapped my ticket to the wheel, spun it, and handed me a small black folder. "Take this," he said. I opened it. An expert piece of spy equipment: concealed within were miniature photocopies of the menu, dessert menu, wine list, tea list. "Write your tickets that way." And his finger struck beside the first appetizer on the miniature menu where in red pen he had noted the proper abbreviation. I looked closer. Beside some of the menu items were adjectives: "smoky," "piquant." I checked the wine list and indeed every bottle came with evocative jargon: "gunmetal," "leather," "oak." It was a masterpiece. Cy could speak knowingly about every item on the menu without ever having once to think. "We're getting slammed. Don't fuck up." I looked up and Cy was already gone and Jennifer elbowed me out of the way to snap a ticket to the wheel and shout out a panicked round of appetizers. "Okay they want this antipasto without radishes, they hate radishes, and they're already in a bad mood — "

Round tray cocked before me, I quickly learned to bullshit, to tell interested faces about whatever smoky or piquant dish they felt they needed my inside opinion on. Some of the dishes I had actually eaten, but, since I had seen how they were prepared, and by whom, I learned not to let my knowledge interfere with my descriptions. The soliloquies I improvised at five were polished by eight. Don't know the menu, know the customer. "Serve from the left, take away from the right," advised Cy as he sped past. Customers pondered thoughtfully, orders filled the air above the tables, tickets poured through my book. In the waitstation, to appease the cooks who were irate at how slowly I was picking up my food, Cy had loaded a giant oval tray with nine plates of my customers' entrees and numerous side plates. I did not see how it could be lifted but my right hand found its center of gravity and hiked it above my head, my shoulder silently screaming at this unprecedented vector of exertion. Moving to serve these dinners, I got dizzy when I glimpsed a party of twelve sitting where two of my tables had been pushed together. Cy appeared and asked me if I wanted him to take them, and I nodded, too weak to speak. I refilled waters, teas, coffees, fetched more drinks, asked if everything was all right, pushed the dessert cart by, fashioned weirdly complicated ice cream delicacies following shouted instructions, put lemon wedges on the edges of saucers, brought extra plates, anticipated future requests, made jokes I didn't hear, read at a glance from afar water levels, impatience levels, empty or pushed-away plates. And I pocketed cash. And twice or thrice poured coffee into a glass of ice and sugar and drained it standing right there in the waitstand, against regulations but I knew no health inspector would dare intrude on such a night — health regulations were for Tuesdays. Cy pounded the metal shelf under the heat lamps and asked the cooks if he could get them any soda, saying it was on him though nobody suspected he would actually pay. I had been working for three hours and hadn't once thought about stealing anything. In these circumstances, I felt that if I stole for example one of the fancy peppermills from the dining room, that karma would be passed directly back to me the next time one of my customers sent me for fresh ground pepper and there was none available. In fact, I considered bringing back the peppermill I had stolen from storage and keeping it in my apron.

In the middle of my section, a plastic fern postured inauthentically where the fishtank once was.

Bing bam boom. As I approached Tom the floor manager I could tell by the look in his eyes that he could tell by the look in my eyes that I wanted to tell him something he didn't want to hear.

"One of the gentlemen at T3 has trapped a cockroach under his water glass."

"What."

Eisenhower's had no windows, an indoor wood grill at the edge of the dining room, allowed smoking and had an ambiance one reviewer described as "Early American Mine Shaft." It was night dark inside even at noon. What gave it atmosphere were antiques. The giant wooden booths were taken from a Pullman dining car. The dining room featured an oak grandfather clock—a seven-day regulator made for the Triangle Shirtwaist company. The mounted bear was an eccentric, rustic touch that appealed to old men and hipsters. The walls were covered with weathered planks salvaged from a demolished barn, picturesque, porous and impossible to fumigate to the depths of their pestilent crevices. I had worked in the kitchen, I knew all about the roaches. The one trapped under the glass was a baby.

"What?"

"One of the gentleman at T3 has a baby cockroach trapped under his water glass."

"Did he see it?"

"He pointed it out to me."

"Did you remove it?"

"I started to but he asked me not to."

"He asked you not to."

"Right."

"He has a roach under his glass and he wants to keep it."

"Yeah."

"Why."

"I didn't ask. Maybe he's an entomologist. Or something."

"Entomologist."

"Oh boy."

Tom vivisected me with a look and went to put on his finest tableside apologia. I chased down a dessert order. Out of maraschino cherries. Need to restock the maraschino cherries. In kitchen waitress in tears over some incident. Up two flights of stairs. Storeroom. Cherries. Down stairs. Desserts.

"We wanted this without green peppers."

"The chef insisted. He said the dish is not piquant enough without the green peppers. Try it. Trust me. If you don't like it we'll make you a new one."

"I'm allergic to green peppers."

"Very well. . . Like I said: can I get this without the green peppers please! Huh? Iain. . . Dude if you just pull out the peppers and send me right back out with it they're going to know. The gentleman is allergic to peppers. Jesus don't threaten me. Fuck. . . I'm terribly sorry sir, they were about to whip you up a fresh order but we have just run out of angel hair. Is there something — " Ba da boom ba da bing. Cy circled his tables like a shark. His tickets went into the red, a carnival strongman every time he brought the hammer down. He saw their desire and worked it. $200 bottles of champagne, seldom served, were decanted and plunged into silver ice buckets. Corks ricocheted around the battlefield; we apologized to our customers. It was bad form to let champagne corks go flying but Cy took a perverse pleasure in this theatrical ejaculation. Cy would prepare Caesar salads tableside with hands as rock steady as a surgeon's, taking his time with the desperately needed salad cart while a row of unseen waitstaff cursed him backstage. He would finish with a flourish by wielding his giant peppermill importantly above the romaine, or he might conjure up a fireball of cherries jubilee. He officiously presented for approval bottles of beaujolais, shiraz, cabernet sauvignon and, upon receiving the approving nod of his patron, flipped out his winekey with the precise purpose of a switchblade in a streetfight and corks no matter how rotten or tenuous gave way to their bottlenecks in smooth pops heard all around the dining room. He never touched bottles to the table nor spilled a drop of their blood on the linen. Cy sold the biggest, choicest cuts of steak, and awaited them by the kitchen window pacing like an expectant father outside the delivery room.

"*Medium*-rare, he said it like. Emphasis on the medium."

"Fuck off, Billy Ray Cyrus."

"Cook this steak to his liking and I'll order you a bourbon and put it on his tab, he'll never notice."

"Bourbon talks, bullshit walks."

"Heard that. Hey Billy Ray, here's your spinach salad. Can I get a Cuervo for that?"

"Cuervo no, house maybe."

"Who the fuck do you think you're dealing with. Do I look like an amateur? Get me a worm."

"How am I going to get you a worm without getting you the whole bottle?"

"There you go. And a lime."

"Excuse me, did you graduate from something today? Because — "

"Because I graduated from draft beer in styrofoam to-go cups. Because it's gonna be a long night. And because I'm either gonna core you — "

"Hey man can we just pretend this is fine dining?"

" — or make you a special dessert tray."

"Tiramisu?"

"Tiramisu, cannoli — "

"Double chocolate torte with — "

" — with Chambourd glaze and white chocolate shavings."

"Nice. I like."

"I get creative when I'm drunk."

"They don't call it a speedrail for nothing boys. When Calvin turns his back, I attack. I want your best baked potato with this prime rib, don't serve me up one of those mealy fucking spuds. V.I.P. customer, I think this guy wants to buy me a new watch."

"The green pepper people reordered. Can I get a rush on this. . .? . . .Hello?"

I was staring at a ticket hashed out in my handwriting, mumbling to match up its inscriptions with the menu items in the window when Cy came up, put a bundled apron in the window that was snatched by eager hands from beyond, and turned to me.

"I'll bet you twenty dollars I can throw a tray from the front door over the entire front dining room."

"Swordfish for the lady, steak for the gentleman. What the fuck is this tapeworm-looking shit? Sure Cy."

"Over the grill. Twenty."

"And pasketti for the brat. Choke on it. Right, Cy."

"Shake."

"All right, all right. Wait, what?"

"Manager is in the bathroom so I'm going to do it now."

For a second I thought he might mean it but the second passed. I shouldered the tray and weaved out past panic-stricken incoming waitstaff, almost losing control of the barge I held above my head. Cy stood by the front door, bow-tied and aloof, arms folded over his tray, and nodded to me. He had a peculiar look. Then he struck the pose of an Olympic discus hurler. A cloud of conversation drifted above the boothtops and seemed to slow such that I could hear every word. A burst of laughter rang out staccato and Cy spun and flung. The clink of a suddenly upset glass of water and somebody saying oops followed by a burst of excited voices and chairs scooting back. The tray went up as must have my eyebrows, my jaw dropping. Excuse me she spilled her water can we get — The tray went just over the rafter. A music of forks on plates, cups on saucers, slow drawling pleasant conversation. There must have been a hundred ways that tray could hit someone's head and injure them if not kill them outright. The word *college* frozen in the air, a ring of glasses raised in toast, cheers, everyone smiling, a flashbulb popping as slowly as a matchflare. Oh yeah I have a birthday in my section T12 the little kid, almost forgot. Cy had spun to halt and stood seriously by the door, dreamily watching over his flock. It passed close enough to a chandelier to make it swing so slightly. If it hit someone would he run? The tray was spinning, losing stability, descending over the glassed-in grill area. "And how's the tilapia?" I could just hear a tap over the crowd as the tray hit the floor behind the bar, ricocheting who knows how among the bottles down there. The bartender was not present and nobody seemed to have seen what had cast a flicker of shadow across their tables. I stared at Cyrus in what must have been shock. He let loose with a smile. "Twenty" was what he mouthed to me, emphasizing this point with a handgesture that imparted the numerals two-oh.

From that point on I had no trouble. I beamed at every table, knowing what they didn't. They had been saved from decapitation, they were all blessed.

In front the last customers started to leave and in back the first employee beers started to tip. I was flushed with gratitude that I had been allowed to survive all that by who knows what twists of luck and reserves of endurance. I bade my last tables farewell like the final departing guests at a family reunion, almost sad to see them go. I accepted their generosity, added their cash to the wad in my pocket, began my full evening of getting drunk while pondering the laminated printout of what seemed like a laughably long list of closing details for my section, a full two hours more work for a man in my condition. I handed Cy a twenty in the breakroom. A couple of the others regarded this exchange with detached curiosity. Cy beamed at me but said nothing. Obviously he required no encouragement. "Still selling blowjobs Cy?" chuckled Iain.

"Save your money, Iain."

"Yeah, Iain, that's your rent money. You need that to buy beer with."

"He should give old Iain a discount because Iain so tall Cy won't have to kneel."

"Now Iain, you go spending your paycheck on head again you really will be in the doghouse."

"Hey. Tonight I'm being good. Two beers. I'm still on my first."

On the breakroom table Cy had set a full forty-eight-ounce pitcher of Double Diamond. Iain raised it and took a swig off the side so long it drew hoots from the crowd that had gathered there by the ashtray.

Calvin the bartender's birthday. The owner home in bed, free drinks flowed furiously in the illicit after-hours club of the restaurant bar, where we sat in a row at the edge of the unlit vacuumed dining rooms beyond, tables already reset with polished silverware, burgundy glasses and fantail folded napkins of lavender cloth. Oban. Kneeling in the same stall where the best lawyers took their cocaine, I threw up more money than I had earned that evening.

In the darkness behind the dumpster, my back to a brick wall, a half bottle of Moet Chandon White Star between my knees, I waited for dawn, determined to see daylight that day.

Workplace closed, locked out of home for another night, fake light permeating the swirling dirty amnesiac air of disreputable pubs, we capsize glasses. The stars we squeeze into drinks, the taps behind the bar are slot machine handles laughing froth. Our new bills, freshly unfolded wings, lift into the air, pay the pub a higher rent. The bartender pilots this ferry to the other side of night, where we disembark. Gravity fucks with us, we dance with nobody, fall.

A stitch of sleep before the alarm clock reopens the wound.

"Jesus, Cy, your apartment looks like a restaurant. Neon sign and all. How did you get the booth? Never mind. I don't want to know."

"When Tom was hired, the night before he was about to take over managing the night shift from Patricia — you weren't working there then — I moved out one of the booths, respaced the others — more leg room, you know — and redid the section map at the host's station. It confused the hell out of the staff. They assumed the owner had it done."

"Nice fishtank. You bastard."

"Don't know nothing about it, boss."

"So it was you. Why'd you let Jane get fired?"

"What are you complaining about? You got her job. How was I supposed to know she'd get 86ed? Since only an idiot would suspect her. Fucking Jane. What was I supposed to do, confess?"

"Yes."

"You think if I confessed the owner would like call her up and apologize and invite her back to work? Remember when the Nicaraguans were fired for stealing the bread maker, and then it reappeared?"

"I do remember that, actually. Pretty well."

"Well, did he apologize to them? Hire them back? Post a retraction? Learn to say *Nicaraguan* instead of *Mexican*? When you're gone you're gone. Old boy ain't sentimental."

"No. Where'd you get the fancy cash register? What is that, brass?"

"I am not at liberty to say, but what is in the cash register may be of interest: cigars. Monterey Excalibur?"

"I'll take a Monterey Excalibur."

"Armagnac?"

"Read my mind. Armag— Armagnac."

"What we really need to steal is one of the owner's cars."

"No shit. Can't you get in trouble for that?"

"Me? Nah."

"I think the penalties are steeper there than with grand theft fishtank."

"They left you thirty-seven cents?"

"I think so."

"Yeah. See, they must have been afraid that, if they left nothing, you'd think they just forgot to tip. Thirty-seven cents says you're stiffed."

"That's pretty much how I interpreted it, yeah."

"So she told you the chicken was too tough and what did you say?"

"I offered her a steak knife."

"Oh man. That's — Oh man."

"Guess you don't do that with chicken."

"I guess not. Yep. I like that Dusenberg."

"That motherfucker."

"That's my boss."

"The Monterey Excelsior — "

"Excalibur."

"Excalibur. . . is tasty."

"Isn't it?"

"I could almost smoke something like this."

"That's what you do with a fine cigar. You almost smoke it."

"Ah. And Armagnac? You supposed to almost drink it?"

"No. Drink it. No, drink it slow. Like almost not drinking it. The snifter collects the aroma, you can smell it. Smell that?"

"Smells like gasoline."

"Oh it's a lot more expensive than gasoline."

"Can you run a car on it?"

"Ah, not in a straight line, I can tell you that."

"Oof. Smooth. No. Ah. I guess that would be unsafe. Did you get this from work?"

"You tell me."

"How am I going to tell you?"

"Aren't you a waiter now? Do we serve Armagnac?"

"Well, let's just see. According to this marvelous little cheat sheet you've concocted here, well, I guess this brand is crossed out. Like a drink so good that when you run out you just leave it crossed off on the menu, just to show you had it?"

"Something like that."

"So. You're a pro. What's the best thing you've ever stolen from work?"

"I can't tell you that."

"What do you wish you stole? What is the best thing possible to steal from work? The ultimate bonus."

"Ha. The profits. And you?"

"The best thing you can steal from work is yourself. That's what."

"I hear you. I think."

"A life that isn't about money at all: not earning it, not spending it, not having it."

"I don't mind not spending money, if there's another way to get stuff. Or not *earning* money. If there's another way to get money. But not *having* money?"

"Why not? It's not attractive, it doesn't taste good — "

"Endless credit?"

"Sort of."

"And you want to steal that from work?"

"Well I don't know where else I could steal it from."

"Maybe working for a credit card company, juggling fake accounts, falsifying records — "

"I don't want to work for a credit card company."

"Well neither do I. I don't want to work."

"Well neither do I. Quickly let us drink to that."

"Amen. Shall I roll us up a stick?"

"Ho. Is that connoisseur grade as well?"

"This? No. This is just busboy."

"To work?"

"To work."

In a dream Cy and I play Russian Roulette. He can barely contain his delight. Each time I take the gun, I am prepared to die, to surrender to Cy. Seven clicks and Cy is still laughing. He knew we could never die at this. I turn around. Behind me in the doorway is Mr. Call-Me-Adam, but his shirt is unbuttoned and I see that beneath his skin instead of organs he is made of cogs.

Cy's truck is parked in the alley around the corner. Three stories up the side of the building, standing on the railing of the fire escape it is possible to reach the edge of the roof, balancing on one foot fifty or so feet above the jagged dumpster maw. Only this part is not a dream. We have been drinking, I realize. Wait, what? Go, Cy says from above, and I throw my chest over the edge of the roof, drag myself onto the restaurant, roll onto my back and lie there. It would be enough, I think, to lie here and look at the sky, on the roof of the restaurant. Wouldn't that be adventure enough? I fumbled out and lit a cigarette. I heard a tinkle of breaking glass nearby and the word *shit*. Without breaking and entering, just to enjoy the evening on top of, literally above, our jobs. Over it. I blew smoke onto the moon.

Quarter moon, someone stole the other seventy five cents. The man in the moon maybe. God owed it him, he works there. Is he lying on the roof of the moon looking up at me too? Why is there no revolution on the moon? If I stare at it can it help me stop spinning?

I got up to look for Cy. Past a broken bottle, through an open window, inside the attic. A shadow moved in behind me to shut the window, brushed past, urged me down moaning steps through a doorway into dry storage. A flashlight came on in my face, then played over the shelves.

"Need anything?" Cy asked.

"I have all this. But, Cy? I don't want to go any further. Cy? I'll meet you outside."

"Let's just drink a shot downstairs at the bar. Nobody will know."

"One shot? No. I'll meet you by the car."

"You can't go back over the edge of that roof. Are you crazy? Anyway I shut the window up there. That way it'll look like whoever broke in was a keyholder, a manager. But they'll never know. If we just drink one shot. We were just drinking there a few hours ago. What are they gonna think? Some guys broke in from the roof to drink a shot let's fucking dust for fingerprints."

Fingerprints? In the beam I saw Cy wore leather gloves. I didn't. Where did he —

But the flashlight was already bobbing down the stairs.

At the bottom the restaurant was black and silent. Feeling through shadows in the dim glow of the exit sign I found my way behind the bar. But Cy wasn't back there. I didn't need a shot. I needed to get rid of this still burning cigarette. I dropped it on the tile and stamped it, kicked it under the bar. Had I left a smudge? I knelt to feel the floor. Then I heard Cy. We just needed to get out of this place.

"Cy. No. I don't want to."

"You don't have to do anything. I already loosened it. Just take one end."

"Cy — "

I was left alone. My mother was a professional strikebreaker and traveled constantly. My father owned a bar and two restaurants and worked late hours. He had a large desk in his den where he did accounting. I used to play beneath his desk when he was at work. It was my office within his office. He kept a shoebox filled with money down there. I would conduct imaginary transactions. Rough stacks of intricate, crinkled bills, adult numbers with zeros, bound with rubber bands. But one day he came home from the restaurant early and found me on the floor of his den playing with his money. He reddened. I had done something bad. I was sent to my room but wasn't punished. The next day the shoebox was replaced by a safe.

All day I lay in bed trying to decide whether to go in to work, call in sick or just disappear. Disappearing would be tantamount to confession, and calling in sick would simply have been obvious. Finally, I concluded that if I was ever going to go back to work at all, I should get it over with. Hung over, infuriated, I went in. Stocking the waitstation, filling the ice bin, icing the cream, slicing the lemons, I moved past Cy in fierce silence. The air was electric. The manager and owner were ensconced in the back office, door closed. There had been, I pretended to learn with surprise, a robbery the previous night. Someone had stolen the stuffed and mounted black bear from the back dining room. Some overzealous zoologist in our midst had struck again. The incredulous faces told me I was not beyond suspicion. For there simply was no plausible explanation for the theft of a bear.

Tom showed up in the waitstation. "Allen wants to see you. And you. In his office." He had pointed at me and Cy.

On the office floor was a stack of boxes containing new security cameras. From behind his desk, where he seldom sat, eyeing us like a man in charge of things, the owner glanced at his Rolex and asked us which one of us should he fire.

My customer wants a hamburger, though the closest thing the restaurant offers is filet mignon. Derek shrugs. With my bowtie on, I leave the restaurant, get in my car, and drive in search of hamburger. In a sprawling empty facility I park by a warehouse. Inside, a conveyor belt is taking deformed cows, some with no eyes, some with three heads, some with no legs, to the slaughter. There is nobody but one man in the corner mopping blood off the floor. I tap his shoulder. When he turns I see the blood he is mopping is his.

Fired. How unexpectedly rock might turn to mud and send you sliding to the base of the mountain. The world hated the wriggling people infecting its clean financial systems. The shock of being fired was stinging, especially from the first job I ever had which paid well. A clamor of fire engines hurtled through dry streets. Singed feathers trickled to earth. Now how I envied boring frightened people, their white button-down shirts, washed cars, pained eyes, zipped lips, internalized oppression and abuse, neuroses, angry spouses, hungry drugwild children, crushing mortgages, grinding treadmills of earning and expenditure, sharp jealousy of the Joneses, being passed over for promotions for years and then laid off with a shrug, layers of television with which they numbed themselves, arbitrary and loveless marriages one phone call to a lawyer away from devastatingly expensive dissolution — all the termites that swarmed their minds while stuck in traffic on I-5. I wanted to be those puppets who jerked through the motions gnawed at by a wonder why doing the right thing wasn't working. I wanted a job.

I circled the ad, called the number, wrote down the time and address. I showed up, stood in line with other losers, signed three forms, had my name checked against a short list of people known to have failed at this job. I was given a map of a wrecked neighborhood and a case of phonebooks. Inspecting the product, I looked myself up but I wasn't there.

Black smoke evacuated a burning construction site, crawled down alleys, rolled over railyards and cinderblock runs, passed through rusted razor wire fences and boarded-up schoolhouses where squatters crouched on grimy sleepingbags and broken cats slid through cracks. Under skies of dirty foam, across a littered ocean floor, I carted my ballast. I shouldered a load of phonebooks in a canvas shoulder bag I had retained from a job delivering newspapers in my childhood, the first trophy of wasted hours. This new loot managed to excite me enough to keep moving. I would have stolen phonebooks for my friends if I had any. Pondering the obligatory cover photo of the Space Needle, I wondered whether the blue sky was airbrushed in. I didn't know Cy's last name. Who would call him anyway? If I crawled faster I could pass him; he would wait on me.

A high tide of commerce in the 1970s had left a high-water mark of outdated typefaces across broken signs on an abandoned mall ornamented with a faded jetsam of futuristic polygons. It held one surviving store.

I walked into Rent-A-Room. Nobody was in sight. Various televisions echoed news through a kaleidoscope of simulated rooms showcasing rental furniture ensembles. I walked through an endless ghost home, telescoping bedrooms opening one onto the next. Shelves displayed decorative books. Curio cabinets housed mock heirlooms and artificial bric-a-brac. A series of framed floral prints masqueraded as an intimate human touch. The illusion of home ended near a ceiling of beams and track lighting, open-ductwork chic. As a dab of realism, a mannequin sat at a small table staring at an open book. When she blinked, I jumped. I saw at her feet a basket of cleaning supplies.

Another employee sat on a couch, boots on the $35.99/month coffee table, rolling a cigarette on a green plate missing from a dinette set. A profusion of dreadlocks cascaded onto his blue vest. And he knew my name.

"Kemp!"

By high school, being an A student had ruined my life. I was a pariah, a target of abuse by zealous youth of all sizes, races and castes. I lived on the bottom. Jasper saved my life: a lot of people who would have beaten me up instead beat Jasper up. Jasper's hulking, scarified slouch gave him the bearing of a thug. But his demeanor ultimately invited rather than threatened violence. From beneath a wide brow his burned eyes stared out and held you in the kind of intense, direct stare that you find only on infants, the insane or people who know they have something on you. His x-ray gaze was unsettling, you could only look at it for so long. You worried he was on dangerous drugs, then worried more that maybe he wasn't. An irate gym teacher tore out his nose ring. Jasper manufactured enemies.

One midnight freshman year as I lay in bed the phone rang once. That was Jasper's signal for me to stuff a mummy of blankets beneath my bedspread, crawl out my window, and creep through shadowy neighborhood streets to the park. Beneath the slide we huddled for protection from the wind and circling police cars. He told me that he had a job in a Freedom gas station. He was fourteen, having lied about his age on the application. From two to six a.m. he sold gas behind bulletproof glass — the graveyard shift — which explained why I hadn't been seeing him at school. The security cameras were all trained on him, he said, he could not steal. So he gave me a shoplifting list and told me to come in while he was working. An hour later I was walking the brightly lit aisles, with wooden casualness examining various items. Into my backpack fell candy, batteries, film, coffee, rolling papers, tobacco, ephedrine, malt liquor, and even a poster offering a toll-free number employees could call to rat each other out for stealing stuff from work. I put a pack of gum on the counter and he rang it up, jabbing the register like a pompous concert pianist. I nodded and exited into darkness overlit by a glowing Freedom sign. It felt good, like shopping, but free, and with a flourish of artistry. It was a forbidden ballet.

Jasper didn't last long working for Freedom.

His mother was a dancer, he said. All that was known about the inseminator was that he left his jacket.

When Jasper reached that special age, he started having intimate encounters with police. He got more action than me. I distanced myself.

The last time I saw him he washed dishes with me for a day. He wandered into the crowded dining room in his marinara-splattered apron, and, to the horror of the customers, smoked a cigarette at a table impeccably set in anticipation of the mayor's reservation of eight. Jasper laughed as the owner dragged him out back and threw him against the dumpster. I promised myself never to help him get a job again.

"Jasper. I didn't recognize you with hair. Wow. You're still alive?"

"Don't ask me."

"Have a phonebook."

"Delivering phonebooks. I did that."

"You're moving up. Look at all this — you got TVs, VCRs, DVDs, computers."

"Like being inside a pinball machine all day. I want to throw myself against the wall until it goes tilt."

"Easy now."

"But I was homeless. They hired me."

"Homeless?"

"Got evicted."

"Why?"

"Writing on the walls and not paying rent."

"Ha. That all?"

"No."

"Where you living now?"

"Well, they gave me a key. . ."

"No. You live in the store. You sleep on that modular sofa?"

"Until somebody rents it."

"Keep sleeping on it, nobody will rent it. I don't believe this. Where do you — never mind. You haven't changed. Except the hair."

"Nope. Still the same. Haven't even bathed."

One night during a thunderstorm, while Jasper was sleeping at the Rent-A-Room, lightning struck the mall. All the appliances — every wide-screened television, all the boomboxes bulging with speakers and ornamented with light — came on at once. Jasper came awake plastered in sweat, paralyzed, as they babbled at him in bad English, fractured Spanish, deep dialects in languages he could not comprehend. What they had to say was something he could not listen to.

After telling me this, Jasper laughed and put out his cigarette on the rental art (New Dimension Studio Red Jazz Nightclub Scene $12.99 / week). "I never liked TV. I thought I had the perfect job when I started living here. Every night kicking it on the Ashley Living Room Group. Then I started getting the nightmares. Never sleep at work. It leaves you psychically vulnerable. If you sleep at work, your boss owns your dreams. When I saw the ghosts, the veil was lifted. Invisible people crowd us. Splinters of soul are lodged in every product. That television has hundreds of parts manufactured by people sweating in factories in distant countries. By watching it, we intertwine our destinies with all of theirs. We have family we don't know about. Somehow the web of human relations has been made invisible to us."

"Hey Jasper, another beer?"

"You go ahead."

"Some of this rental stuff isn't bad. You get commission?"

"I talk people out of renting. People can't afford to buy, so they pay more to rent."

"Well, you've gone beyond anything I've dared, living here. What if you get caught?"

"What if I don't?"

"Hey Jasper, what's it all about?"

"Oh shit. It?"

"It."

"It is not all about furniture and video. This I know."

"From my own experience I can say that it is also not all about fresh ground pepper, mahi mahi, or Kendall Jackson '82. Not that I'd turn any of that down."

"There's always PBJ."

"And PBR. And it's not about phonebooks. Now phones — the kind that take MRIs and microwave burritos and program the weather in Tokyo — maybe. But phonebooks, no."

"Nah. People get excited about gadgets because they confuse that stuff with something else they crave. Some need so basic there may not even be a word for it."

"You're saying what it's all about is unsayable?"

"Think of it. If that got out, that what people crave, money can't buy? That's a major paradigm shift. The Earth wouldn't be flat anymore. People would quit their jobs."

"Is that what you want?"

"Yeah, that's what I want. Even just to imagine that. Back in high school I thought that what I wanted was to fuck shit up — "

"Easy now."

" — but it's not that, it's fucking shit up to get it out of the way, to get to what comes next."

"What comes next?"

"Say you're walking at night on the wrong side of town. And out of the shadows somebody walks up to you. Do you smile? Do you run? Do you think about whether you have a weapon? Do you say hi? The answer to that is what comes next. You decide."

"What would you do?"

"Probably I'd be the one coming out of the shadows."

"Then I'd definitely run."

"Then that is what comes next."

"Fuck that. Hey Jasper, what's the best thing you ever stole from work?"

"Explosives."

"From where?"

"Construction site."

"How'd you get a job doing construction?"

"I didn't say I worked there."

"Hey Jasper."

"Yeah what?"

"You ever kissed a girl?"

"Fuck off."

"All right. Now I have to know, where's — " but it was too late. I stood up, knocking my beer onto the video game console, and tried to make it out the front door into the night before I made a mess neither of us would be in any shape to clean up before the store opened.

I got my paycheck, paid a reconnection fee to get water again, but miscalculated. The check bounced, and I owed both the bank and the water company a fee. The water company required me to pay this fee in person on the other side of town. I paid bus fare in pennies. I maxed out a credit card to get a cash advance, using half the advance to cover the bounced check, half to pay the credit card bill to enable future cash advances. I was out at a bar drinking the change when, back at my apartment, my water was reconnected. I had left the sink faucet on. My basement apartment was flooded, turning the unpaid bills scattered beneath the mailslot to pulp, ensuring more disconnections would ensue.

How many cities have I lit up with the friction of my treadmill? I imagined I was born a poolhall prince, buried in my genes the information of a savior. I itch to shed my self. Simply put, we were meant for something better.

I funneled the leftover phonebooks into a dumpster and walked into Rent-A-Room. The dollhouse was starting to look lived in. A stale stillness hung over scattered newspapers, Chinese take-out cartons, overflowing ashtrays, beer cans, scraps of wire and cleaning products. I whistled into the furnishings. In response came Jasper gliding through the store on a skateboard spinning a thread of smoke from a cigarette hung on his lip. He slalomed around some easy chairs to the front door and locked it. He pivoted the board so it pointed into the store, gave me a nod that said to follow him.

He had pulled a wardrobe from a wall and uncovered a door leading into the empty mall. I followed him through into a ruined temple of commerce. The mall had fallen and was now an evacuated, gutted carcass, dim light seeping from a broken skylight where pigeons fluttered among dead monocular security cameras. Some stores showed no sign of ever having existed, others seemed to have been abandoned overnight, yellowing signs announcing sales curling in their dusty glass facades. Near the center of the structure were enormous double doors large enough to admit vehicles. I followed the fluttering tails of Jasper's trenchcoat as he rolled down sweeping corridors past these empty cages. Some echoing back stairs led up to a wide and flat roof where Jasper kicked through ducts and aerials to the edge where the sun was setting. A halogen popped reluctantly on over the desolate parking lot. I noticed loiterers around the metal corrals where shopping carts were once parked. I wondered whether they would give me trouble when it was time for me to walk home.

Back at the bottom with Jasper. Not a happy reunion.

Planted in unlaced combat boots, jaw jutting out, a garden of stubble wandering his chin and cheeks, Jasper studied the sunset. He grabbed some air in his fist. I recognized his spasms. Something in his wiring made his synapses prone to shortcircuiting. His neurons glowed redhot from resistance to their own messages. At these times he couldn't speak, when he opened his mouth out spewed a torrent of sparks. Long ago something had crawled in his ear and curled up to hibernate in his skull. Now and then it would wake and feed by chewing slowly through his brains. In high school he got in trouble for going in the girl's bathroom and dropping a burning butt in the trash where it ignited a smoky conflagration. But he wasn't trying to be disruptive — he needed a smoke and had been busted too many times in the boy's room. In chemistry lab he had no patience for the experiment the teacher was explaining, and, while his lab table looked on uncertainly, mixed the substances until he achieved an explosive effect. The room was evacuated and he was saved from punishment by an ambulance. Touched by these destructive wonders, he became motivated to study. And became a stellar student. In chemistry.

We surveyed the downtown skyscrapers. I didn't know if we liked them. "Plans," he said, "we have big plans. To turn the city upside down and shake the yuppies into the sea. Some of those buildings we can keep. Redmond is going to the bottom of the mountain, though." He stuck his arm out to arrange the skyline by hand, a florist perfecting a bouquet. "That's fine with me," I grinned. He met my gaze but was not smiling back. Without taking his eyes from mine, he shook a cigarette out of his pack and held it to me. I hesitated before accepting it.

"Light?" he said. He held his Zippo over the edge of the roof, and tossed it into the air. Surprised, cigarette in my mouth, I just managed to catch it before it fell to the parking lot. He smirked.

At night we sat in the store playing a video game. Behind us a constellation of softly glowing table lamps hung with price tags stretched into the distance like buoys at sea. I was startled to see a deranged person staring in through the window. When I pointed him out to Jasper, Jasper put down his joystick and went to unlock the door. I thought he was going to scare the vagrant off, but instead he stepped back to allow the homeless person, and a couple other people who had been sitting against the wall, to shuffle in. One of them stood by a laundry machine, removing his clothes. The others disappeared into the store to find beds.

It seemed like a good time for me to leave.

Who did he mean by we, I wondered, walking across the parking lot.

> Now that you are sixteen, and legally able to work, your mother and I have decided to terminate your allowance with this parting gift of one hundred dollars in travelers' checks. You are now a productive member of society. Congratulations.

My childhood had been spent mowing lawns and delivering papers. At sixteen, my first adult job was fast-food. A gourmet burger stand. Cornishons instead of pickles, capers instead of relish, romaine and radicchio — no iceberg. Dijon mustard, and sun-dried tomato paste instead of ketchup. "Shredded steak" instead of "ground beef." The *pommes frites*, it was implied, were pureed by hand in olive oil. We offered, among other specialties, a beet burger, veal burgers (marsala, parmesan), a caviar burger, and a truffle-quail burger with prosciutina.

Working the counter, I addressed the customers with mock sophistication, affecting an English accent.

"May your burgers be more exquisite far than mutton, ivory or eggs."

The laughing trio of college students went out into the night. I locked the door behind them. "We're closed," I shouted to the kitchen. Silas the manager appeared in its doorway, licking a joint. He cocked his head toward the business office. I went to punch out. After our business meeting, I cleaned the bathrooms, while, before scraping the grill, he cooked us both absurd burgers with everything.

Silas disappeared and was replaced by Dave. Or maybe his name was Steve. He was a stocky ex-marine with a big moustache, proud about being a recovering alcoholic. His bearing suggested that he commanded respect, an expectation I had difficulty living up to. One night I was describing our "shake list" with faux-seriousness to some customers. They were delighted, but Dave or Steve was enraged by my levity. He bellowed, "We're going to talk about this later!" but we never did. It's strange, looking back, to realize that, up until that moment, I had actually enjoyed that job. But never again.

I began to pocket the toy prizes they included in kids meals. Bright, colored, goofy plastic monsters. In my room, they were a band of mutant technicolor rebels, rallying on my computer table. They were wild things and there was no question but that we were going to stick it to the man.

Dave or Steve didn't last long. He had some kind of relapse and started drinking openly at work. He showed me his tender side, which was even worse than his mean side. One night he was in the kitchen sobbing so loudly about the regional manager that the customers could hear him. He was replaced by yet another manager, to whom I had to explain the workings of the restaurant.

Dave or Steve had cleared up any misconceptions I might have had about enjoying working. I had seen the inconsequential job crush him and everybody who had to work under him. I became a poker face. I was a soldier in a war against mediocrity and I didn't know if I had any allies. From then on, I was behind enemy lines all the time.

You enter into a cynical relationship with the job from the moment you apply. It doesn't hire you, it hires itself. You have been selected because of who you are not, who it will make you pretend to become. Lying is the first responsibility of any job. You lie at the interview when they ask you why you want the job.

Jasper's friend Hunter needed help stealing stuff from work. Hunter was a musician and seemed nice for a thief. He had horn-rimmed glasses, sideburns, a striped shirt and talked fast.

In the dark behind a university athletic field he studied a giant ring of keys until he found the right one to unsnap a padlock and admit us into a shed. He flipped on the lights. In the sudden glare the punchclock seemed frightened, surrounded by hoes and spades, as if the regiment of implements had been murmuring intentions to turn on it. Hunter pointed at wheelbarrows, trowels, shovels, and we piled them into the back of a pickup, securing a tarpaulin across the top. We drove into the forest of Snohomish County. The night air was cool and sweet. Jasper slept against the window and Hunter drove. I sat between.

"You're a groundskeeper, I take it," I deduced, "or were."

"No. Programmer. Musician. My friend Ella was a groundskeeper. But she was injured on the job so they fired her. She kept the key."

When he met Jasper, Hunter explained, he was still a graduate music student. One of the members of Hunter's jazz ensemble invited Jasper to sit in with them on partially dismantled AM radios fed through a series of effects pedals. Hunter was unconvinced by Jasper's chops, but they remained friends.

The strapped music students were charged by their department for photocopies of sheet music they were expected to learn. One Friday evening before the building was locked, they entered the office wearing white jumpsuits, adhesive moustaches, hair tucked into baseball caps. Carrying clipboards and speaking loudly about an imaginary basketball game, they unplugged the copy machine, and, casting cheery greetings to a night custodian, rolled it down the hall, into the elevator, onto a loading dock, and into a van.

With unlimited copies, their ensemble was better able to promote its shows, copy charts, and send out press kits. They got a gig in a swank penthouse lounge. A floor-to-ceiling window behind them offered a stunning view of downtown Seattle and Puget Sound. Clad in black ties, they uncomfortably reconstructed standards. Before them at a bar made out of glowing glass bricks, candlelit yuppies talked to each other on cellular phones. They were offered the restaurant's storeroom as a place to change clothes and tune. After their set, when they found out how little they were getting paid, they retired to their dressing room and filled their coats, instrument cases and bags with china, silverware, crystal. They tried to make it to the elevator without clanking.

We crunched onto a dark gravel road and rattled through deep ruts up a hill, parked, and killed the engine before a dark farmhouse, where in the afterimage of the headlights a shutter hung askew from a single hinge. A light came on and a woman came outside chiming "*¡Hola!*"

Jasper and I unloaded the equipment.

"These tools were going to be used to beautify university flower gardens for students to litter in. But my friends will use them to grow food."

My work could be anything: waiting tables, building pyramids, fighting crime, writing. I run around doing things I don't want to do but the agony is that I want to be running around doing something else, to surrender to ideas, struck, open to beauty. I truly want to work. When work means, as the philosophers say, in the best possible way, play.

Delivering phonebooks to businesses, I hit back doors. I preferred to meet the workers without customer relations skills. Jasper came along, apparently leaving his store unattended.

My route took us through a park. He tossed his cigarettes onto a sleeping homeless person he knew by name. He ducked into a store and came out unwrapping a new pack, though I didn't see him pay for it. I wondered what kind of glue would hold the city together when money stopped working.

Walking down an alley past an open garage door, we were stopped by the scent of cannabis. We looked at each other, nodded, and walked in. A cavernous bay was lit by a lattice of grimy panes and a few bulbs hung from hooks. A trench in the cement floor allowed access to the bellies of vehicles. The walls were slung with a rubber slaughter of belts and innertubes. A clanking crept through the space. In the back of this hangar a red articulated city bus stood— two halves joined by a flexible coupling — metal entrails scattered about it. I saw feet protruding from under. We walked over and stood by the feet. For a moment I wondered whether we were looking at someone who had been run over. Jasper coughed, the clanking stopped, and the feet slid out from under the bus propelled by the body and arms of a mechanic lying on a platform squinting up at us. Her jumpsuit bore the name *Barb*.

"The new phonebook's here," I remarked, holding one out, feeling a bit ridiculous. She stared at me to see if I was for real, then pointed at the floor. I set the book down among the ratchets, shrugged, and we turned to go.

"Hold on," she said, sitting up on her wheeled platform. "Do me a favor. Go look at the taillights. I need to test these turn signals." Behind the bus I passed a flask to Jasper. A blinker came on. "Left!" I shouted. And again with the right. The brake lights flashed. She came around back and I held out the bottle to her. It was like watering a flower, she brightened at once. "Works. C'mon boys. Let's take it for a test drive."

We followed her up the steps into the bus. She arranged herself in the cockpit and I stood beside her, hanging on a pole. "So you just got done fixing it up?" I asked.

"Yep," she levered the door closed and fiddled with the display so that the bus read "out of service." Jasper walked to the back. I offered her another shot which she knocked back and, wiping her chin with a cuff, cranked the motor to life. Lights flickered down the length of the bus. Headlights lit up a rack of motor oil on the wall. "How long have you been working for public transportation?" I asked, just to have something to say. She pulled a joint from her pocket and stuck it in her mouth.

"From fifteen years ago until yesterday." She lit the stick and put the bus in gear.

We swung onto the boulevard. Traffic seemed to part for this whale. Cars swam beneath our windows. We looked down into the set frowns of commuters up against each other in another traffic clog.

She ran a yellow light, sweeping through a fast left turn that swung me from my pole, and glided to a stop on hissing pneumatic brakes at the next intersection. I looked down through the windshield of a police cruiser. The two cops appeared to be singing along to the radio, their faces enacting great sorrow. Barb raised a hand in acknowledgement of her fellow civil servants.

"I can't go back to that garage. A friend works there and his boss comes back tomorrow. Any idea where I can park this?" Barb asked. I looked back at Jasper, who was looking back at me.

I have never paid for toilet paper.

One of the best drivers on the crew, Barb had missed a day of work when she discovered her daughter was pregnant. The father was her boss. She had a long talk with her daughter, convinced her to get an abortion and they smoked a joint together. The next day she had been asked to take a "random" drug screening. Knowing there was no way she would pass, she arranged to kidnap a bus that was awaiting repairs. She had been the perfect employee, city buses were her life, she no longer exactly felt like she wanted or expected to live. And she hadn't thought about what to do with the bus, she just knew she couldn't give it up. "Child, you look at a map of the bus routes of this city and you'll see where I've been these past fifteen years. Give me a blank sheet of paper and I'll write you out the schedule, exactly like the printed schedule except for a couple places where mine will be more accurate. I've dealt with blown gaskets, flat tires, knife fights, junkies shooting up in the back, drunks throwing up in the front, bums pissing in the middle, shit, blood, kidnappers bringing their victims onboard and straight-up flat-out psychopaths who don't know whether they were on the bus to Spokane or a train to heaven. I know more about running a municipal transportation system than my boss, my boss's boss, my boss's boss's boss and the mayor — especially the mayor. If anybody knows more than me about buses then that person is God, but these days God takes a cab. They wanted to cut the lines that serve the factories and the ghetto but I told them they'd be cutting their wrists because you can't run a bus system without no passengers. One time in '99, when the protests were going on, they decided the buses should be for delegates only, nobody who might be a protestor, which meant no working people at all. So me and my girl Joanie, we figured out a system to take all the sparkplugs out of all the buses. It took three people and twenty minutes and we might do it again. We also sketched out how the whole fleet could be driven away in the middle of the night and those plans still exist. Now they want to tell me to piss in a test tube and tell me I'm not safe to drive? No. This here bus is mine now. I don't know what I'm going to do, but I know I earned it."

The city bus stood in the mall corridor, articulated around the ghost of a corner chocolatier. Telling me these things, Barb moved a ladder over its hull, peeling, repainting, prying off bits and pieces, removing identifying marks, scattering scrap across the orange-tiled mall floor. Jasper was lost in thought, walking in and out of the bus.

"That could be your next home," I suggested.

"I'll have to remove some of the seats," he responded absently, chewing his lip. He was hard to joke with.

You move deeper into the city; you move deeper. Under people standing on the shoulders of people standing on the shoulders of people. The spreadsheet of skyscrapers, each window a cell, is an edifice as immovable as our money problems seem. Nobody believes they can crawl out from under a hundred-story bank, but those monuments can be shrugged off as easily as feathers. Money is at most paper, no more than a bribe and threat, an imaginary negative number.

Life on the installment plan. We didn't ask to be born, but the world has sold us this body that must be repaid. We inherit servitude. We must pay back our lives faster than we can live them. And the debt moves between all of us, grit in the gears, tarnishing our esteem, corroding our relations, doing inescapable damage to our dental work, marriages, automobiles.

All of this is presented as a wealth of opportunity in a country where anybody who is not crippled by an indolent character can swim gracefully upward through social classes to a position of comfort and prestige. There are a handful of examples, well publicized. But for every billionaire's million is an unnamed person with a fatal illness who must choose between death or debt for life. During this sentence, millions of people will be charged by their banks for not having money. This is a system designed for the rich to rob the poor of more than they can ever have, and charge them extra for having been robbed. Imaginary numbers, nothing else.

My father put me to work on the lawn when I was too young to wonder who got to decide which plants were weeds. As soon as I was old enough to command minimum wage, he hired cheaper illegal immigrants for the yardwork, and sought only to get me out of the house so he could rent out my room.

I was accepted into the university, so the summer after I graduated from high school I applied for student hourly positions. I worked in a cafeteria and the library.

The cafeteria was in the basement of the student union building. It had burrowed itself into the tunnels of that basement decades earlier and the legacy workers seemed ancient. A very old man washed dishes, living in a room of steam where the conveyor belts that brought the trays and dishes from the dining room emptied out. Old women and men with no apparent connection to university life tended the kitchen equipment. In the locker room I stood silent and miniscule among old salts, once again a puny high school freshman among giants, trying not to be noticed. There was an old-fashioned punch clock and a sense of being in prison. I was supposed to wipe the tables after the students and staff got up to put their dishes on the conveyor belt. After a week, I went next door to the bowling alley and played pinball. Within a year the old cafeteria would be gutted, its full-time employees scattered to the winds to try their luck finding jobs at places like Denny's, and the whole basement was refashioned as a food court sporting a handful of sad fast-food chains.

In the library I was taught the rudiments of the computer system and learned how to check books in and out. I was permitted to check books in and out to myself as well, and nobody checked to see whether the book had been returned. I think I realized the implications of this the moment I was trained to do it. I checked out many books and records. They were all checked back in. The documents library was located inside the secure bookstacks, a catacomb of books where only graduate students and staff were allowed access. It was easy to slip away from my post shelving documents and retrieve rare books which, outside of that building, I would never otherwise hold. I could stow them on a carrel of reference books, where they would be perfectly camouflaged, push the cart out of the stacks and hide the books I coveted among the dictionaries on the public shelves. After my shift I'd go collect them.

The stolen books and records burned my conscience. I wrestled with whether to take them back. After all, it was a public collection, there for everybody. Nobody was profiting from their sale. I was stealing from myself in a sense. But I could not help it. I would steal them and make myself return them to a bookdrop.

Finally I announced to my library employer I was quitting to take a job at a restaurant as a dishwasher. Two weeks notice. My compulsion to steal from a decent job at a good library forced me to punish myself through taking a demeaning job in a kitchen. But not without one last binge. On my last day, I discovered in the back of the employee-only part of the library shelves of uncataloged records, not yet officially in the collection. They did not exist. I had no choice, overwhelmed by compulsion. Working furiously, I assembled a small collection, and, on my break, went out through a discreet side door. Sweating for fear of running into another library worker, I rode the elevator to the basement, left through a basement door, tucked my haul into my car and returned to work. My theft included a moon landing documentary record, *Sounds and Ultrasounds of the Bottle-Nose Dolphin* and a Timothy Leary record whose cover was a purple spiral with the enormous letters *LSD*. I listened to it; it was totally stupid, but priceless.

I didn't last long as a student at the university.

There were too many panhandlers on the street for any to make an effective bid, so the crazies campaigned for change while the sane ones sprawled against the bricks scowling. Cars idled at the traffic light. The drivers did not look over but their windows glided up and you could hear the soft click of doorlocks.

Behind the cracked glass of a newspaper machine, headlines reported that the best jobs to be had now were in the weapons industry. I leaned in to read the visible portion of the story. Due to the proprietary secrets of bombmakers, employee retention was sought. It was possible to major in mass destruction at certain forward-looking universities. Standing up to ponder this, I saw that I was standing in front of a business. Everybody liked a free phonebook.

The used bookstore was almost invisible from the street. It had one hand-scrawled sign that read HOFFMAN'S and another that read HELP WANTED.

Stacks of books climbed to the ceiling beside overloaded, sagging shelves. A bald head floated above a counter, round spectacles perched on an aquiline nose. The brisk, diminutive, sharp and serious clerk waved away the new phonebook. The cheap paper offended him, he preferred the older edition. His eyes roved nervously over the spines on the walls when he spoke.

The application asked for three favorite novels and three references. I lied about the references.

This professorial clerk, my new manager Tom, was younger than me but seemed older. Behind the facade of fallen storefronts on that row some unschooled architect had made creative use of the uneven margin between an office suite and a movie theater to create this sprawling store. Variously constructed shelves zigged and zagged through tight corridors and tiny rooms, and every shelf had overflowed into piles on the floor. The whir of an overwhelmed dehumidifier harmonized with the buzz of light fixtures that came on in a cascading arpeggio across the ceilings when he flipped the switch. Showing me around the claustrophobic bibliographic labyrinth, Tom pointed out all the books that were his — a section apparently misshelved beneath history, in the employee bathroom a tower of erotica, in the broomcloset Egyptology stacked to the ceiling. He had developed many interests since beginning work at the bookstore. A freelance researcher, he followed footnotes.

"I used to take books home. I ran out of space in my apartment, even learned how to build bookshelves out of books. When the previous manager was fired for stealing money and I was promoted, I decided just to keep my books here in the store. I'll buy them someday."

"So you steal books," I smiled, adjusting to my new employment situation.

"No. Not anymore. They're mine, but I leave them here. So it's not stealing."

"But there's nothing really to stop you?"

"Well, would you stop me?"

"The books aren't inventoried?"

"Would you want to inventory all this?" he gestured, knocking over a column of paperbacks.

"Does the owner. . . ever. . . work. . . here?"

"He's in Portland. He makes his money doing something else. Possibly the store is a tax scam. He emails me to sweep whenever he feels that nagging pang of authority."

"And do you?"

He gave me a serious look. "I'm glad you're motivated. The broom is behind my Egyptology. I can't find the dustpan, so I've just been using these old *Playboys*. They attract customers, we need to get rid of them. Sweep, you'll be employee of the month. You can sweep?"

"I can even mop."

"We don't have a mop. This isn't a hospital. I'm going back to work on history."

He picked up a book.

When the workplace became our own, we worked harder and got less tired. We fell up, grew young.

I dropped out of the university and for a summer subletted and temped. I was sent from place to place, doing clerical work, catering, groundskeeping and asbestos removal; plundering supply cabinets, breakrooms, tool sheds, janitor closets and whatever anonymous desk I was seated at for the day. Nobody knew me.

An industrial-size sack of cafeteria rice, a typewriter, liquid paper, mechanical pencils, varieties of tape, boxes of pens, window-cleaning solution, clipboards, photocopies, coffee filters, a telephone, a computer, an interesting ashtray, a ball of string, two white jumpsuits, a stapler labeled "DO NOT REMOVE FROM 3RD FLOOR COPY ROOM."

I thought my grandparents demonstrated cowardice by working one full-time job their entire lives, joining unions to protect positions they complained about. I can see now the value in the fact that their jobs were *theirs*. Years later, the model was for everybody to have multiple, disposable part-time jobs. The expectations that came with full-time work — survival, security — were thus thwarted. Your failure to make ends meet was due to your moral weakness, addiction to daily sleep.

But things turned around again. No more would I have a better job so that I wouldn't have to have a worse job, or have a worse job to avoid being turned down for a better job. I would collect as many as possible.

At the end of my first week at the bookstore, Tom was surprised by my suggestion that we get a drink after work. His reaction confused me; I wondered what else there was to do after work.

We sat in the corner beneath a cigar store Indian. Tom shook his head sadly over a rocks glass. The idea I had been trying to impress upon him had at first left him unconvinced, even twitchingly perturbed. But after another round, we were, I felt, only a couple of shots short of a breakthrough. I sent him back to the bar. He moved as purposefully as a professor ferreting out a call number.

Hatcheted from an enormous piece of wood, the looming chief glared onto the miscellany of TVs, video golf and bowling, Tequiza mirror, darts, Guinness clock, Redhook canoe, rotating Budweiser Chippendale snowscape, mounted marlin, popcorn machine, Harley-Davidson leather-clad couple slowdancing clumsily by the jukebox. In a headdress of feathers, wielding a tomahawk, brow furrowed in studious indecisiveness, he paused, realizing himself outnumbered. The rich northern forests and mountains he was poised to defend were already impaled by an obscene needle.

Tom returned with a round of carbombs.

I found that agreeable. "Something to take the edge off."

"That edge is the only thing propping me up."

"That cigar store Indian is offensive."

"Yeah it is. It's disrespectful to Native Americans."

"It's disrespectful to workers."

"Yeah. How?"

"That that prize is sitting here and nobody's stolen it yet."

Tom wandered out on the dark street and stood with his forehead against the cool glass watching me stuff into the tip jar a dollar bill scrawled with the words *Steal That Indian*.

I steered him back to work, where we stood with stiff, counterfeit nonchalance on the curb unlocking the bookstore. A car drove by but it was neither police nor anybody familiar. "Working late," Tom muttered, fumbling with the keys as he rehearsed slurred rationalizations, "I came back because I left my bag at the store."

"Me too," I concurred, "I left a lot of bags at the store."

He giggled and dropped his keys.

"I'm working overtime," I suggested, "to help make room on some of those shelves."

"Shelf help."

We stepped in, the door clinked shut behind us and we peered into the blackness, scarcely able to believe the owner wasn't lying in wait. Through the red glow of the exit sign we moved into the rows, each with an empty cardboard box. Five-finger employee discount.

In the silence my ears discerned sibilance. It seemed the authors were whispering. All tumbled onto the sagging planks of this ad hoc archive, they barely figured into the system, history of thought collecting dust. Was it their ghosts I heard? Or were there other book thieves here conferring in other rows, ranks of unseen scholars moving in the shadows between shelves, fingertips telling titles on spines: *Capital, Down and Out in Paris and London, Working, Revolution in Seattle, Grapes of Wrath, A Troublemaker's Handbook, Nickel and Dimed, Confessions of a Union Buster, The Seattle General Strike, Gig.* How many of these books were written at the author's dayjob, stolen from work by actuaries, physicians, admen, lepidopterists?

After browsing our way up to the third floor, Tom used his key to disable the alarm and we left by the rear fire escape, clanging down steep metal steps clutching libraries to our chests. "Taking out the trash." I wondered whether any policeman could ever suspect us of stealing old books.

When I got home, my trophies on my wheelbarrow table, I was ready to leave. I thought I'd hit three jobs in one night. I had disabled a restroom window latch at the phonebook center. It appealed to me, this vision of the night city lit from within, in closed places of business where employees worked surreptitious overtime, a secret nightworld in which Jasper and I would steal a forklift and drive it to Cyrus's apartment, break in, steal everything he stole. I had a box of hot thought and didn't give a fuck.

I hadn't seen Jasper in many days, and set off to find him. Down a brick street where nervous men loaded a pool table onto the back of a truck, under a track along which a passenger train clicked slowly, across a barren concrete valley where a three-wheeled shopping cart lay on its side beneath a humming cluster of halogens, the stores were dark except for Rent-A-Room on the corner. The wide-screen TV in the window flashed a diagram of a microorganism beside a mushroom cloud. I walked toward it across the pantomime of light it splashed on the silent pavement. Cut to an animated map of Asia. A red splotch over coastal China directed outward by blinking arrows to other Asian cities. The screen started to blacken. Flames rose up all around. In the window the television was on fire. I stopped walking. A sharp flash vaporized Asia.

When something important happens, it is over before you have a chance to react. For the rest of your life you either pick apart the memory until it becomes a memory of a memory, or you stay in that instant forever. You have caught a glimpse of the infinite, the possible, through the rifts in the understanding you have cobbled over things. Stealing the bear had been like that. Cy had showed me a part of something that was true and knew no maximum. If I could go back in time, I would have stolen the fish tank one hour before Cyrus arrived to steal it, just to fuck with him.

I threw my arm across my eyes as the TV tube exploded through the shopwindow. A wincing bang rebounded from buildings opposite, glass particles rained across the parking lot. There were copies of everything, the world flickered. Then all was silent save for a crackling wall of greasy fire in the shell where the store had been. I shook the glass out of my hair. Flames crawled up the walls and danced on the roof.

In the light that spread through the Rent-A-Room I saw no furniture. It was empty. I walked to the mall's double doors and peered into the caverns, already feeling the heat. There was no bus. The fire raced down arteries in the floor. The whole mall was going up.

I gathered Jasper had just quit his job.

When they died it seemed they were cut off midsentence. The phone rang and I somehow thought it was them, perhaps calling to tell me something to make it all right. Not the voice reporting the accident. I don't know what they would have said, only that I am still waiting for someone to say it. They left me nothing. There was no will, and banks moved in to gobble up any extant assets. *Why me*, I would have asked, *I wasn't the one you wanted*. I guess I kept wanting there to be somebody there, somebody to help. But there was never anybody there. I had stolen from them too, but I hadn't stolen enough.

I was scared we were wrong, scared we were right, scared of the consequences of bringing these shadows to light. War is war, whichever side started it. At the end of his first week at the bookstore, Jasper walked out carrying an encyclopedia. Tom watched him go, peering from behind stacked crags of new arrivals, both of us silently wondering why Jasper didn't have the decency to deceive us — to hide the book in a backpack or ask the manager whether he could *borrow* it. Tom looked guilty. I felt foolish, as if, by not engineering a deception, Jasper was undermining my technique. The moment passed. Tom returned to separating the new arrivals into two stacks — one his, the other the store's. I shouldered my full backpack of discreetly secreted books and followed Jasper to Emma's. There was the relief of the first beer.

"Hey Jasper if you're looking to blow up a bookstore, go get a job at Waldenbooks or Hallmark or some shit like that. Okay? Do not torch Tom's store. I was trying to help you out, getting you a job there."

"And I appreciate the job. And the place to live."

"You mean you're — Shit."

"Hey, my house burned down."

"What section?"

"Last night it was fiction. But I couldn't sleep. I think tonight I might try economics. The old elevator shaft has access to the roof. I might sleep there if the weather stays dry."

"I thought you told me not to sleep at work."

"This is different."

"How?"

"At this job, we don't really work at work."

"True. So what did you do with the Rent-A-Rooms?"

"Took them to the farm. My friends and I are getting organized. This is wildfire. Together we could steal back the world."

"It was never ours."

"Oh yes it is."

"I used to have friends like you. But they got me in trouble."

"Oh we're going to get you in trouble. You can meet my friends tonight."

A bottle broke. Somebody clapped. Time passed. Hourglasses of beer elapsed. Swarms attacked the dartboard. Butts accumulated in little mountains. Peanut harvests were eviscerated. Pinball warriors rose and fell in digital symphonies.

And then I recognized my former coworkers Derek and Iain at the bar drinking blonde German beers out of tall glasses each hung with a lemon wedge, and with a pang I recognized Cy's money. Derek was laughing. Iain saw me in the mirror and raised his beer, nodding respectfully. I sensed I had become legend.

Cy sat down at our table.

"Evening Jasper."

"Cyrus."

"Mr. Kemp. Long time no see?"

Reflected in his glasses a video poker machine pixeled a montage of cocktails and dice. Half his mouth smiled.

"You two know each other?" I asked.

"We do."

I tried to level with him, though it wasn't my specialty. "Cy, man, I mean, I don't know what to say, running into you here, like this, because, I, like, wanted to be your friend, but I hate you."

Cy turned across the room to Iain and raised three fingers, mouthing the word three. Iain hailed the bartender and put tequilas on Cy's tab, unperturbed, waiting on the waiter.

"Did you plan that I would get fired so you could steal a freaking bear?"

Cy's smile hung on. The other side of the mouth started to join in. "It had to be you. If I took the fall the whole restaurant would cave in. You know I do half the work up there. Man, I'm sorry. I didn't think it would go down that way. I'll give you half my tips for the next two weeks."

"That's a start."

"The next month. That's cool that you want to be my friend — I don't think anybody's ever said that to me. You get a free subscription to veal."

"Cash is fine."

"I'll let you have the bear."

"Fuck you."

"When I fence the bear I'll cut you in."

"Yeah you will. When you find that fucking black market taxidermy underground. Meanwhile I lost my shot at making some decent money."

"You can get another waiter job. There's plenty of hooks in the sea."

The bartender had come to distribute our shot glasses. Cy tapped each of ours with his, and drank. Jasper followed suit. I set mine down without drinking but didn't let go.

The bookstore is a castle built into a cliff overlooking the sea. Lightning rakes the sky and waves pound the walls, flooding the children's books section. The tempest is getting worse, tides are rising, the lights are flickering. I am collecting books I want, planning to escape. Tom is furious with me. He is the manager and cannot leave.

It was night and I was walking with my phonebook bag down a steep hill. Skyscrapers blazed in the darkness, floors of empty desks stacked to a sky patrolled by helicopters. Inside these bright and empty architectures a few custodians and night watchmen made rounds. In alleys I saw workers carrying crates out of doorways, stacking them in vans. The city inside out. Maintenance and sanitation ran the largest skyscrapers, at night performing necessary services in nearly empty buildings devoid of idea guys and exec VPs. Certain diners had peak business hours after closing.

There were no cars save a few taxis, their drivers talking on phones and seemingly uninterested in finding fares. As I knelt to tie my shoe a bus pulled up to the curb and its door hissed open. I stood to wave the driver on. Jasper was in the cockpit grinning from beneath a cavalcade of dreads. I sighed and stepped on board. He threw it into gear. Barb and a few other passengers sat near the back. Most of them I recognized. It seemed to be a meeting in progress. As the articulated bus turned a corner, they slid out of my view and back again. I made my way down the aisle.

Cyrus was speaking, leaning into the aisle from his seat. I knew he could sell a thirty-dollar fish, but I had no idea the little twerp was an orator.

"I'd pace. I'd walk to the door of my apartment, stop, walk back, sit down, get up. I was deeply conflicted, possessed. I knew I had to break into work but I tried to fight it. About three a.m. I let myself into the restaurant. And I discovered I wasn't alone. In the kitchen I found Jasper up there at the grill, lit cigarette in his mouth, cooking himself a steak, drinking rail gin out of the bottle. I was all set with a story for what I was doing there. But this fucker had no story. He didn't even work there. He had been fired that evening, his first night."

I remembered that night.

"He was supposed to get a meal with his shift, but was fired before he could get served. So he broke and entered, and didn't even touch the cash register or the office. He cooked steaks and I fixed drinks, and we had dinner, lit a fire in the fireplace, got to talking. That was the first meeting of this club.

"See, stealing stuff from work is something everybody knows. It doesn't matter who you are, what you do, whether you take money or paperclips. You steal from work like water flows downstream.

You have to scratch that itch. Well we're not here to admit we steal from work, we're not here to stop stealing stuff from work, we're not here to understand why we steal from work, we're just here to get better at it. We got a few new faces here. So tell us who you are and what you stole this week."

"I'm Jeremy. Antique, wooden cigar store Indian. Boss was furious. Policeman who filed the report was one-quarter Suquamish and three-quarters unimpressed."

"Erica. I'm redoing my house and needed some copper pipe. Next time somebody tries to use that basement sink they might start to figure it out."

"Dirk. Matte cutter. Expensive tool. Useful in mounting my lithographs."

"I'm Matt. I work as a valet at an expensive dinner club. I've stolen linen napkins, glassware, pitchers, teapots — basically a whole dining room."

"Todd. I was mopping the store and cleaned up a CD player. But I got caught and fired."

"My name is Nick. I've been making Steal Stuff From Work zines and using the company bulk mailbox to send them out. A memo was posted that seemed to pertain to my activity, so I hid the key to the bulk mailbox for a week so nobody could use it. That shut them up."

"Derek. Security cameras. Some I took home, one I installed in the owner's office."

"Good work. So we've all noticed we're at the wrong end of the paycheck. When we work, we pay. Our wage is just our change. Stealing stuff proves we exist. We can decide which side of the screw to be on. And it's right. It's perfect. We're on to something. We're balancing the scales. Hey newcomer, tell us why you're here."

"I'm Kemp. You just got me thinking. Remember the movie Flash Gordon? I saw it as a child and again as a teenager on my first acid trip. It must have made an impression on me. In the movie, Dr. Hans Zarkov is brainwashed by Ming the Merciless. Zarkov is strapped to an operating table, fitted with a metal headband, and a giant device is pointed at his skull. But Zarkov resists the procedure through the pure strength of his mental will. When the brainwashing begins, he recites to himself multiplication tables, mathematical formulae and even the lyrics to an old Beatles song.

He pretends to be brainwashed but his big secret is that he is still himself. This is what having a job is like for me. The job is a form of psychological reconditioning. It cuts you off, immerses you in an environment where you are forced to believe in it, abducts you and demands your loyalty. Thinking about stealing things engaged all my mind in an activity that ran counter to the job's indoctrination."

"Hey everybody. I'm Hunter. We've stolen from work. That's the first step. But we could be doing more. Each of us stealing for ourselves can bring home a bit of loot over time. But take it to the next level, and start stealing stuff together? Stealing stuff for each other? Stealing stuff for people who don't work? If we pooled our resources, we might live that dream of not having to work, not being scared to get fired, not being on the run from birth to death. Nothing can happen without work, no money can be made. If we share, then together we own everything. Also, Jasper has been in touch with other like-minded groups working on other things and they like our ideas. We've decided to make November eleven Steal Stuff From Work Day. A secret holiday for pranks, sabotage, grandiose thefts, surfing the web at work or just calling in sick."

"Every day is Steal Stuff From Work Day."

"Ha. For pencils. But I mean inside out, stripped to the walls."

"Why not steal the walls?"

We had stopped moving. I stood up. A police car, lights dancing, had pulled us over. A couple of cops climbed onto the bus. I saw one of them raise a palm and thought Jasper might have pulled a weapon. But before I could make for the exit, Jasper gave him a high five. The other cop smiled and flashed us a peace sign.

If we lose our jobs we might be unable to afford to go to the hospital — they had that on us — but it was back on them because we couldn't afford the hospital or a life worth living. So we had nothing to fear, and if they couldn't frighten us, and if it was too little, too late to bribe us, we weren't working for them in any way. The cool wind blew sweet into our sour, stifling cubicles, those beige burlap crates with walls that could not be decorated because tape would not adhere and thumbtacks could not penetrate, beauty-proof boxes in which we hunched like eggs in a carton, rotting in our shells. Time our taxis took to the streets. A red bulb in an upper window of a building meant the night staff was in and the game was on, the building was won and those within were on our side. Anymore we'd walk the city and see our blood burning on every rooftop. Fleets of limos and taxis and towtrucks with red flags flown from the aerials. Any of them were friendly and could be flagged down. At night owners and management fled to Mount Vernon and bedroom communities to fester in million-dollar shacks whose housekeepers had already copied the keys. We all went about the same aching jobs but they no longer hurt us, we were all smiling now, free. When the sirens blew, when the cruisers lapped, we felt at home. It was our city.

I always had a secret I could not tell — that I despised my job. By stealing from work, I had a more interesting secret. I was active in the game, rewiring the rules. I wasn't sure I liked Jasper's club. I liked my secrets. My secrets were my power. I did not want to know that everybody had the same secrets.

We had started hanging out at each other's jobs. In the afternoon, Cy brought brandy to the bookstore for breakfast. That evening I dropped by Eisenhower's for lunch. From where I sat smoking on the back steps, through the kitchen door I could hear the owner holding forth in a foaming tantrum, railing about soup. His white Lexus was parked beside the grease pit, illegally blocking the alley as was his custom. Cyrus stepped out, handing me a sandwich, laughing a cigarette out of a pack. "So we're slammed, right. It's tense, but manageable. Then the owner shows up. Just dropping by to grab free coffee or whatever. Sees that people are waiting for their food. He storms into the kitchen, where the cooks are just flying to get the orders together, and he tells them to stop. He lines them up against the wall, and he tells them they're doing their jobs all wrong. He says, 'We're going to take it one ticket at a time.' And, real slow, he pulls. . . down. . . the first ticket. Squints at it for awhile, you know. He has no idea what the abbreviations mean. Just stands there trying to fucking decipher it. Which makes him even madder. He makes Iain work on ticket one while the others stand around."

"So it'll be awhile before your food's up."

"Yeah it will. And ticket one turns out to be a bowl of French onion soup, which could have taken all of a minute to prepare, and then he finds out we're *86* on croutons, down to the last two bags. So what does he do? He flies into a rage and stomps on them. Derek had to put his hand in hot broth to calm himself."

"Did he wear a coat?"

"Did he what?"

"Did he wear a coat, Allen, the owner."

"Oh — this is great — and while I'm standing there, pouring orange juice, you know, giving my tables free drinks so they won't kill me for taking so long — "

" — with their French onion soup — "

" — yeah, French onion soup. He calls me over, and he tells me I'm not putting enough ice in the orange juice. Like we don't have enough else to worry about right then. I don't put ice in juice.

We're serving the fresh-squeezed, not Tang. Up to here, he says, four fingers, he says, because he has to pay for his son's college education, he says."

"— and you're wondering who's going to pay for your college education."

"I look through the window and the cooks are still lined up against the wall, awaiting further orders, laughing at me. More ice. That's a six-dollar glass of juice. I cannot believe that man. Thinks he knows how to run a restaurant. Punish the employee for not punishing the customer. The only way I'm gonna get a college education is if I steal it."

"Did he wear a coat?"

"Why does he have to pretend he knows how to work? What is it with you? How should I know whether he wore a coat? What difference does it make?"

"If he wore a coat, maybe he left it in the office."

"Maybe he did."

"Maybe he left his car keys in the pocket."

Cyrus stared off.

"Or the coat rack, if he came in the front." I offered, helpfully.

Cyrus pulled intently on the cigarette, suddenly a man with all the time in the world, at peace with things.

"Grab me the toolbox while you're in there," I added.

Cyrus's cigarette arced into the garbage and he went back in to work. By the time he returned, it seemed as though the trash can were starting to smoke a bit. "Cut a hole in the coat pocket," I suggested, "so he might think he dropped the keys outside."

Cyrus seemed to regard me with what I took to be respect. "Not bad."

"Take my knife."

"I got knives. Then I'll ask him to show me how to brew a cup of tea. You know, tell him I want to make sure I'm not giving them too much hot water. So his son doesn't have to end up working in a restaurant. That'll buy you twenty minutes right there."

"Tell him you saw a towtruck. He knows he's not supposed to block the alley."

"Nice."

The evening was brisk and smoky. In the parking lot I switched the owner's rear license plate with one belonging to an identical

Lex. Half an hour for the boss to discover his missing car and call the police, one hour for the customers to leave in the other Lexus, half an hour for them to be pulled over and accused of being car thieves, and for the wrong plate to be discovered. So perhaps two hours of driving time. I slid behind the owner's wheel. The leather upholstery smelled like vanilla cigar smoke. I twisted the key and the engine murmured awake. *System active. Looking at this screen while driving can result in injury or death.* I studied the proliferation of features for the emergency brake release.

I put my hand on the wooden gearshift, coaxed it into drive. I was a circle 240 miles in diameter. Whistle while you work. By two a.m., the Lexus was in a barn at the farm.

The steam of boiling coffee turned the gears.

The weight of the clouds pushed our moods out like shapes from a cookie press. In our kitchens, neglected shrines of our well-being, stacked dirty dishes were a monument to our humiliation. There came a rumbling thunder as the acids in our stomachs adjusted themselves. The frustration distilled in our bodies, seeped out our pores in its pure form.

All of us broken, stained, poisoned, crippled, beaten — after work carting our injuries and sins to the meeting place. Sitting with sprained limbs and fractured minds, pooling what remained of our fire to do something about it. Blinded by our walls, circumstances, unable to think except about how we hated our jobs. We didn't necessarily like each other. The thing was our backs were against the wall, we were going down. We were all going to die scarred, that was unavoidable, but what was regrettable was that our lives would get worse as our jobs sanded away our brightness, our creativity, our aspirations, inspirations, fingertips, ears, eyes, sex. We wouldn't just be broken, we would be boiled, consumed in our totality before our scraped shells were cast aside. This is what made the ache in our stomachs like an indigestible bone lodged there, the sheer hatred expressed toward us by no agent we could see. Decks stacked against us had to have been stacked by somebody. The system was too convincing, just so imperfectly designed to contain, defile us, file us in folders and down to stumps, not to have been engineered by bad people. But there was no face we could put to it.

So if we would be buried with scars, let there be scars on our knuckles.

Tendonitis, carpal tunnel syndrome, a new white button-down shirt with a fatal inkstain after one day's use. We drag these injuries to our meetings, things the job has taken away from us permanently in exchange for its temporary money. Fighting to stay awake over a field of zeroes and ones, is consciousness a flame that can be smothered for good? We come to the meeting to blow on whatever coals still glowed in our skulls.

Not everybody is like us. Some fit their cubicles like limp clowns bouncing on sawn-off springs in a broken jack-in-the-box, and lap up those paychecks like August dogs chiseling dried ice cream off a dirty sidewalk. Maybe if we were all just paid more, we would never have woken up to test the strength of our chains.

I didn't know what was going on. The idea kept piling people on top of us, iron filings to a magnet. Talking about it lanced a boil, drained a poisonous fluid that built up in us every day while driving to our life prison sentences, guilty and already fired. It was the only salve for our cuts, burns, fractures and abrasions. When we saw that our solo juggling act was part of this grand and glorious circus, we couldn't resist putting the sparkle back with new moves. Our thefts became less sloppy because our work contributed to a larger art.

The problem of theft went beyond what companies ever let on. Their budgets for security were largely to protect against their workers rather than to protect against outsiders, despite whatever shareholders were led to believe in glossy annual reports in which staged photographs of happy employees stood in for what the companies could not admit looked more like a frighteningly well-organized and hostile army of saboteurs, already through the gates, ready to do bad things. We had joined a war older than most countries. But thieves rule, by definition. While the company ruled publicly, we ruled privately. We outwitted their corporate science time and again. People who believe in each other are stronger. When we got thieves talking to each other, we tipped the scales. That is how our group made a difference.

With Tom in charge, the store bought more books than it sold.

Incoming: a shopping cart of textbooks salvaged from trashcans by a homeless man, useless books we bought out of pity and stacked before the entrance in the free pile that attracted graduate students. Then around this barrier came oversized architecture books pilfered by a custodian at Borders with whose case Tom was familiar. The man bade us a warm farewell, tucking cash into his jeans. But before Tom could even peel the telltale pricetag from his new Bauhaus compendium, the door opened and he moved onto what was left of the showroom floor to direct the landing of boxes of glossy esoterica brought in by a professor known to systematically request and sell desk copies of expensive academic titles, one of Tom's favorite people in the world. Striated paper mesas grew around us, a sedimentary archeology of knowledge. We worked all afternoon to create weeks' more work of pricing, hefting and shelving, and the store had dispensed many hundred dollars more than it had taken in.

"Our work creates more work," I noted.

"Same for the authors. Especially these guys," Tom waved at the academic titles, which I surmised was now his pile. "I just hope my paycheck doesn't bounce again," he growled, counting what remained of the master's money, preparing to secure it in the unwarranted safe.

"What time is it?" I asked.

"Closing time."

"Really?"

"Rounding up to the nearest hour."

Squeezing in the door before Tom could lock it came a man in a pink polo shirt hefting with both arms a brandname-emblazoned racquetball bag stuffed with an implausibly diverse collection of shiny books on every topic from ikebana to building an airplane to germ warfare, as well as a great many scientific journals.

"Where's virology?" the customer asked, pushing his sunglasses onto his head.

It took me a second. "Mr. White? I didn't recognize you standing up."

"Oh call me Adam. You're not at Eisenhower's anymore. So, you're moving up?"

"Sideways. Tom?"

"Yeah?"

Tom was already elbow-deep in the racquetball bag, absorbed in a book about mitochondria. I realized he was actually going to buy for the store unsellable scientific research that would block the biology aisle forever. I found myself further intrigued by the machinations of this manager who spared no effort or expense to prevent us from doing business.

"Hey Tom, do we have a separate section for virology?"

He snorted. "Of course. This isn't an airport bookstore. Virology is in science, which has overflowed into religion. All the way up both flights of stairs, turn right, go past literary biography, Slavic, music, down the small steps, third aisle on your left, you'll see a sign that says Political Science. Go down that aisle all the way to the back of the store. Look for Bibles. If you find yourself in a broken elevator with a bunch of science fiction you've gone too far."

Adam White pulled his wallet from his slacks, thumbed out a card and handed it to me.

"I asked Cyrus why you weren't working Fridays anymore. He told me you quit to pursue an interest in animals. I'm involved with a project in cooperation with the biology department at the university. I had an employee walk out on me today. Do you have enough jobs? Want another? Cyrus told me I should hire you, that you'd be perfect."

"What's the job?"

"Other duties as assigned. And web development."

"I don't have much professional experience with that."

"Perfect. I hate working with know-it-alls."

He turned to the canyon of books where Tom was last seen. "I'm not trying to steal Kemp."

Tom poked his head above some mysteries and seemed to consider whether this information warranted an interruption in his paragraph.

Adam White jogged up the stairs.

PREVENTING INFORMATION HIGHWAY ROBBERY

- Occupational theft
- What employees steal
- Why employees steal (false assumptions)
- Monitoring employee theft
- Punishment
- Backlash
- Prevention

Occupational theft has its origins in feudalism. Though the problem is not new, in the Information Technology industry, it assumes a new character. Since stolen information is usually not lost, only reduplicated, the most significant commodity your technical workers steal is their own attention.

Note that occupational theft is distinct from corporate espionage and arguably more serious, inasmuch as a corporate spy still has allegiance to the corporate world. Occupational thievery, while not as damaging, demonstrates a more dangerously unacceptable disobedience.

Your employees might jot an email to a friend, glance at news headlines, or listen to the radio online. An extra window open on the computer desktop displays an auction whose moment of termination is rapidly approaching, in front of it a large spreadsheet is frozen in the middle of a data-entry task. A dialog between friends scrolls jerkily in a small rectangle which, with the touch of a key, disappears behind a half-finished graphic that allegedly requires hours of fine tuning before its creator's tenacious design intuition can release its hold on the problem. All the while the employee will continuously and instinctively create the illusion that he or she is devoting all his or her attention to his or her assigned task, on a state-of-the-art computer wired to a high-speed network, routinely appearing to work unpaid overtime, in many cases performing in his or her assigned tasks as well as or better than his or her peers. In a flurry of activity, paper pours out of the printer and photocopier, mysterious computer work is accomplished, late hours are worked. Their desks face the doorway so their monitors cannot be observed from behind, and they favor cramped private cubicles over shared office space of higher quality. Such subtleties as text-only browsers allow them to surf the web without telltale colors, graphics, or the conspicuous burst of sound that accompanies some websites — audio clips generally not in keeping with any imaginable clerical activity. It is even possible to write or download software that allows the user to maintain two simultaneous desktops on the same computer — one work, one play — and to switch between them at the stroke of a thumb. An employee, especially a skilled liar for whom pursuing a private agenda while on the clock is a deeply ingrained reflex, can get away with much in the way of leisure unwittingly sponsored by your organization.

However the real danger is not leisure, but rather that the employee will work on an unauthorized project, for another employer, or, worse, for themselves. When the phenomenon known in the discreet IT employee parlance as "multitasking" (what the French call *la Perruque*) is perpetrated by a seasoned worker with a personal agenda, it can be a fearsome force.

There are many false assumptions your employees may hold. They may think that limited use of company resources, such as an emergency phone call, is excusable. They might feel that the company owes them time to pursue their personal life at work if they have spent the previous weekend working at home. They might think that what matters is how well they do their job. And the uncomfortable fact is that they may be right. Many computer workers still consider themselves professionals and expect to be treated as such. Their skills may in fact be hard to come by. This is due to a temporary fluctuation in the market caused by the rapid proliferation of technology, and the problem will take care of itself within a decade. For the time being, you may be forced to compromise your desire to fire. Like it or not, if the employee meets and exceeds expectations, you should think twice before calling him or her on the carpet for having written that lewd love letter on his or her company email account, brought to your attention by security, and circulated among a circle of senior managers, who deliberated the magnitude of the impulsive text's betrayal of office protocol.

While employees holding false assumptions like those above are legion, what may be the most dangerous is the valuable and effective employee with no demonstrable attitude. This type, the chronic obsessive-compulsive vocational kleptomaniac, may be more widespread than we know. Corporate psychologists speculate that there exists among professionals an identifiable cycle of overachievement, burn-out, resentment, theft, and guilt, followed by overachievement, and so on.

Today's workplace has gone beyond the drug tests and security cameras of previous decades in developing electronic means to monitor employees. Every keystroke, every action across the network, even inactivity, can be logged and automatically brought to the attention of the employer. The solution to the problem of occupational theft does not lie in detecting it — it cannot be hidden. Neither does the solution lie in punishment. If occupational theft could be stopped through punishment, then the problem would have been solved in the Middle Ages. Studies have found that, in the largest corporations, where the policies about monitoring employees may be the most intrusive (those companies where security policies are dictated many layers of administration above those affected), concerted efforts to stem workplace theft may in fact exacerbate the problem by provoking employee ire.

Even in a clear case of abuse, how do you measure these indiscretions: in hours or in megabytes? Our principle is that the amount of time or data matters less than the intensity of thought. The danger is not that the profiteering employee will steal objects for their value, reducing the assets of the organization, but that they will use your telecommunication and network resources to pursue their own noncommercial agenda. Distractions such as online television schedules will not seriously disrupt the employee's work, but a genuine intellectual pursuit may command a disproportionate share of the employee's attention.

We suggest that the best way to prevent occupational theft is by proactively striving to eviscerate employee thought. Rather than put the employee on the defensive through overt disciplinary measures, instead foster a workplace environment where the life of the mind cannot be sustained. Disrupt concentration. Reinforce a climate of disinterest through platitudes, corporate language, and the use of non sequiturs. Play commercial radio. Do not openly encourage creativity or personal initiative even when it appears to be to the advantage of your organization. While you will certainly want to pay your employee as little as possible, working is not an ascetic or spiritual pursuit, and should not be described as such. In fact, it is in your best interest not to encourage spiritual development of any kind.

Attached please find a list of strategies, culled from vast amounts of data. Studies have found, for example, that fostering a materialistic mindset by discussing with your employees luxury items such as cars, gadgetry, and vacations is effective. While the pursuit of consumer goods may appear to pose a distraction to the work at hand — indeed buying things may appear to be a passion — in reality consumerism makes the employee more dependent on their position and, as a result, a more conscientious worker.

Many managers have learned from experience that changing the subject abruptly can be an effective means of disrupting any conversation that might be dangerously thoughtful or stimulate the workers' interest in the extra-corporate world. We have found, though, that a shrewd manager may take this technique a step further and nurture employee ambivalence by introducing a stimulating topic, then dropping it. Try talking about politics, for example, and, when the employee starts to appear engaged, change the subject to buying shoes. Virtually all television programming is appropriate to discuss, and television in general has been found to be highly conducive to employee indifference, materialism, and even punctuality. To inculcate the proper mindset to perform adequately at a corporate task without the intensity of thought that can lead to a full-blown intellectual pursuit, there may be no healthier practice than regular television watching. Also attached are a list of popular celebrities, films, and magazines that experts consider ideal topics of conversation to implement an atmosphere of lackadaisical indifference. More advanced variations on these techniques entail using such positive thinking slogans as "The world is what you make it" — not to promote optimism and cheer so much as to discredit the idea of "reality." For a long time we have let our workers know that their contagious dissatisfaction with their jobs reflects only their poor attitudes, not the nature of their work. Carried to its extreme, this method can train employees to doubt the evidence of their own senses.

All people are smarter, swifter, more capable, passionate and decisive than they appear at work. The better your employees do their jobs, the more power they have over you.

Four hours this time but I couldn't quite sleep. Dreamed error messages keep bringing me awake. Inanities passed behind my eyelids with no cessation.

Absurdly early in the morning, gin-asphyxiated cells screaming, I arrived late again, wanting to grab people and shake them. I passed between clenched white walls drizzled with torturous fluorescence. The cruel stupidity of a poster of teddy bears almost brought me to tears.

My desk framed a detritus of notes and scraps, a box of Temple of Heaven Chinese Green Special Gunpowder, and a computer. Orange network cables climbed the walls in duct-taped clusters. On a white board, dry-erase marker arrows flowed from fluorescent post-it to post-it, bifurcating in complex corporate pseudo-concept mapping. A row of empty cola cans were lined up like spent shotgun shells beneath an indoor window offering an aspect of a dull nether-mezzanine peopled hourly by transient undergrads between classes. Twice a year, around the equinox, this window provided an hour of midday sunlight from an alignment of skylight and heavens. Swaying over the laser printer, held aloft by helium balloons printed with birthday cakes, a large inflatable mylar Mickey Mouse leered at me. It had lost pressure in its head and its sunken face was asymmetric and depraved.

My ergonomic chair awaited: time to run around sitting down. I booted up and brewed water.

Stoked into a dreamlike caffeinated tachycardia, I entered my screen. I got it to work, broke it again, and fired semi-comprehensible bug reports up the chain-of-command where higher-ups walked the shaky tightrope of their faith in me.

I lost sensation in my legs.

My first full-time job was not something I had looked for. It's not what you know, it's who you know. Maybe. Or maybe my new enthusiasm for work gave me a glow attractive to employers. Or maybe money itself had become sentient and fully controlled the people who worked for it according to motives we would never know.

My body was still riding its computer desk, mouse hand posed in midclick, but my head had swiveled to attend to my new boss Mr. White. Posed in the opening of my cubicle, he was telling me what had been discussed at the meeting. I had actually been working and was awakening from a trance. In my mind an unfinished house of cards would collapse if I took my hand away. I didn't know how long he had been talking to me. It was casual day. He wore virgin blue jeans, with sunglasses pushed back onto his head — an infuriating accessory given the absence of sunlight in these catacombs. Finally he paused, inspecting his notes to see whether he had filled me in on every last action item. I opened my mouth, he cleared his throat and continued.

"Well that's about it. I don't care for the blue, they don't like the orange. We've almost decided on a text. It was a great meeting. We tried some creative thinking techniques. Got some adjectives here, let's see. . . We want the homepage to be welcoming, impressive, complex, to the point, elegant, futuristic, flexible, austere, old school, contemporary, reliable, innovative. . . To suggest mobility, flexibility, reliability, wisdom, youth. . . We're thinking in terms of the excitement of a waterfall but the solidity of a glacier."

My phone rang. Adam smiled expectantly. It rang again. The house of cards collapsed. I reached for it. "This is Kemp. How may I direct your call?"

The sound of a crowded dining room. A voice with something on its mind. "We're on. Meet us behind the music building at ten."

"Hi, uh, honey," I said, "I may have to work late tonight."

I heard a rude comment made to someone who laughed, and a click.

"Okay," I said. "Thanks. Bye."

Putting the phone back carefully, I maintained an aura of professionalism. "So. We've got a multimillion-dollar research project involving the university, the government and a corporation. The details of the research are not going to be revealed to me, I've got to make a website for it. Without content."

He looked at a pager. "That's a good way to put it. Content. I like that."

"That's — Okay. I'll try to do all that. I — I guess I thought it would go more smoothly. I mean, the site goes live at midnight Monday morning and it's, what, six Friday night and the page isn't built yet. I mean it's built. We've built it many, many times. But it's not to the customer's liking. Or one of the customers."

"Well, you're new here. I thought you might bring a fresh perspective to the problem. Again, I told the university people you thought you should be present at the meeting, but. . . it wasn't possible. Some of the research we're doing. . . is a little touchy. To tell you the absolute truth — "

"Sure?"

" — it's secret. It's — yeah. See, I've already told you too much."

"So I'm supposed to build a webpage to promote something nobody is supposed to know about. Even me. Especially me."

"You know, just take it easy, you can stay here all weekend if you have to. Time and a half. Just. . . try to have fun with it. You know?"

"Let me write this down. Glacier. . . waterfall. . . fun. . . I was wondering — What happened to the person who was handling this project before me? Maybe they might have some insight."

"Well," Adam screwed his face into a euphemism, "she was sort of a temperamental artist type."

Behind Adam a haggard martyr appeared, Dilbert t-shirt tucked into belted shorts hung with blinking gizmos and keyrings, glasses so thick that in their margins one could see refracted the taut stub of ponytail that strained his remaining hair. He was not hopeful.

"The server keeps crashing and the vendor went under. Their phone is disconnected. We can't get the site up and running by Monday."

"We have to. We're giving a presentation to the board Monday afternoon. We can't reschedule. The conference room, the catering, it's all set. We gotta launch."

The programmer padded away on sandled socks. Adam strode off in the opposite direction, my briefing having ended as inexplicably as it began. I had a lot of work to do, in a short time; nobody knew what it was.

It always took him half an hour to leave. I had programmed a simple timer on my computer. I set it for thirty minutes.

"Sorry," I rehearsed softly, "My computer crashed and destroyed all my work."I opened up the design software with the draft of the business card to be left in tip jars.

Steal Stuff From Work?
Confess Your Sins
Email ssfw@stealstufffromwork.com
& Join Our Club
Steal Stuff From Work Day is November 11

I saved the file and uploaded it to our website, where our nationwide network of Kinko's employees could download and print it, distributing cards to local clubs.

"I just remembered," Adam reappeared. Not moving quickly enough, I closed the design program and turned to him. He gestured apologetically. "I'll be leaving for California tomorrow to make some arrangements. It's not clear when I'll be back. So, have fun with this. As long as there's no content we'll be fine. In fact, I just had an idea." He snapped his fingers and looked up at the teddy bears. "A logo. Make us a logo. We'll show them a logo. A mark."

I opened my mouth. "I'll get right on it," it said.

"Okay." He winked. "Don't make it too. . ." his hand stirred the ether for another adjective, a chartreuse post-it affixed to his index finger.

"*Meaningful?*"

"Well. . . We don't want it to be exactly meaningless either."

"No? Okay. *Explicit?*"

"Yes. Okay. Good. *Inexplicit*. Or. . . We'll tell them *open-ended*. Perfect. I've got to get to Eisenhower's before the rush. But call me if you need anything. And I'll see you — next week. I think."

I restarted the timer. Sometimes we would do this all night.

Half an hour later, in the storeroom, the security camera watched me open cabinets until I found a stack of blank CDs, a box of envelopes, a ream of paper. "Working late," I told it. "Just grabbing some things I need to finish the webpage." I pulled a stack of mailing labels off the laser printer, held them up to the light to make sure they had printed correctly, and left.

Gasoline prices were still getting worse. We smoked in the shadows of a loading dock — Hunter, a custodian named Erica and I. Erica was tall, dark and handsome, lanky and restless. With her crewcut, black leather, flannel and jeans, she was comfortable with making men uncomfortable. The alley went downhill where, across a busy street, on a concrete island, bathed in a halo of hospital light, stood the single operative gas pump at Freedom. Idling SUVs lined up around the block to wring petrol from it. Anonymous motorists behind tinted windshields waited to pay one dollar per mile. Inside the station, the clerk was conducting these transactions, each worth more than his weekly paycheck. Cy reached the front of the line, paid for a paper bag, and met Jasper outside. As they crossed the street toward us, their argument preceded them up the hill. Cy was offended.

"I want Steal Stuff From Work Day to be huge."

"It's going to be huge. I'm still going to move tha you turn the treasury over to the local groups."

"The local groups steal their own — "

"Hey!" I yelled, "You thieves want to set up a neon sign? We got work to do here. I just saw a cop car down the hill."

They mounted the steps to the loading dock.

"Got beer?" Hunter asked, unperturbed.

"Check. Let's see this machine of yours," Cy responded.

From a huge ring Erica brought to light various keys, worked one in the back door, snapped on lights. The five of us threw cigarettes into the alley. An orange ellipsis trickled down the slope.

Down an institutional corridor, through another locked door, in the long low basement room where the music school stored recording equipment, Cyrus set the paper bag down on a table. Hunter pulled from a shelf the device he wanted. Cyrus reached into the bag and pulled out a gallon of vodka. Erica's eyes widened, she spoke Russian to it. I pulled the printed labels out of my backpack.

"I load in the discs and we wait," Hunter said. "In a few minutes we'll have one hundred CDs. Jasper, can you explain this again?"

"These discs have ten minutes of silence, followed by loud music. We go to stores that sell CD players, put our disc into one, press play, turn the volume up all the way, and leave. It's a punk-rock bomb with a ten-minute fuse. When it explodes, the employees go to turn off the music and find a label on the CD with a note about

Steal Stuff From Work Day. It's a way to get their attention."

"Whose idea was this?" Hunter wondered.

"You got something better to do?"

Hunter patted the bottle. "Nope."

Crack, swig, glug, pass. Exhalation of vapors, aspirant curse of appreciation.

Erica fingered Jasper's jacket. He eyed her uneasily from beneath his dreads. She pulled on his collar. "What is that? Vietnam War vintage, flight jacket? A G4? You know you can get those cuffs fixed. Want to sell it?"

"Not really. It was my biological father's."

"Did he serve?"

"I don't know."

She punched his shoulder playfully. "Well you must be proud of him."

"No."

"I collect leather jackets. And motorcycles."

"And you're a musician?"

"No. I work for the university. I change fluorescent light bulbs. I'm the fluorescent light bulb guy. That's how they divide things up. I'm the only one who will do it, because a lot of it is a highwire act, climbing out beams thirty feet above the auditoriums. Most of those maintenance guys are pretty old, they don't want to do the scary stuff. I'm not going to do this forever. The university is big enough that I can sit in on classes without getting noticed. And I know some people who can arrange to get a diploma printed up, and can get me in the database to show I've graduated. So I'm getting my degree fair and square, even if I'm not paying tuition. In the meantime, I do the job nobody wants, so I have job security. And keys to every building. Even the president's mansion. And I get bored. It's a stupid job. I get tempted. I come up with ideas. The school, I mean, it has everything you can think of, lots of stuff that never even gets used."

"Stealing from school isn't the same as stealing from corporations," I mused.

"It's sweeter," said Jasper.

"The school gets state funding. You're stealing taxes, not profit."

"You pay taxes?" challenged Jasper.

"Oh? Are you also opposed to soldiers stealing weapons from work? That's tax money."

"I hadn't thought about it," I admitted.

"I have." I wasn't sure I wanted to know what Jasper thought about.

Hunter changed the subject. "Anyway we aren't stealing anything tonight. Erica, would you get fired if you got caught duplicating CDs?"

"Yeah. But who knows how many months it would take for the paperwork to go through. It's a civil service position. But let's keep our voices down anyway."

She was interrupted by song.

We cracked a double door on a small auditorium filled with shrouded pianos. In the glow of the exit sign, Cy had rolled one tarp back and was playing and singing Jacques Brel's "Amsterdam," undone bowtie hanging down his tuxedo shirt, suspenders at his sides. He wasn't bad.

The piano was an ancient Steinway grand on brass wheels. Even with five of us, it was barely maneuverable. Erica slid the rattling loading dock door up. We faced the night, flanking the piano like pallbearers. Cy stood in front, put the bottle on top, flipped open the keyboard guard, struck a low note.

"Stop that," I hissed.

We leaned. Brass casters swiveled to follow the barge into the night. The moon moved across the hinged lid. A ramp descended to the alley before us. A honk came from the bottom of the hill, someone gunned an engine.

"The biggest thing anybody ever stole from work," gloated Cyrus.

"It's Erica's job," I said, "she's the one stealing from work."

"We can't lift this, we'll never get it in the truck."

"With five of us? We can lift it, right Erica?"

"S'just a little music box. Don't back out now."

"How are we going to get it down the ramp?"

"That's the easy part. Heave ho."

We heaved the heavy piano over the edge. It tilted, lurched, rolled. Finding himself in its path, Cy hopped up, knees plinking on the keyboard. The Steinway reached the bottom of the ramp and pirouetted down the hill, Cy kneeling on top, cigarette in lips. The bottle broke on the ground. Jasper and I ran down the ramp after Cy. Erica leapt from the dock. Hunter shouted. I ran alongside the obelisk. My fingers slid over its curves, unable to find purchase as it accumulated momentum. Headlights in my eyes threw a crouching Cyrus into silhouette. At the bottom of the alley, red lights danced atop a police car which had braked to appraise the juggernaut bearing down on it. The cruiser reversed, tires squealing, through the corner of a garage. The siren chirped. The hurtling grand bit off its turnsignal in a bright spray of glass and shot across the street, bent pedals scraping a wake of sparks. Cyrus flashed through headlights, crouching, arms outstretched for balance, still smoking.

The man filling his tank did not see the piano hit the pump.

Blossoming flame bucked the frame out of the piano and the roof off the pumps, everything lifted into the night. A wave of percussion passed through my skeleton. Metal shrieked, wrenched from its moorings. A second fireball erupted in an incandescent afterimage. The massive piano frame came down onto the hood of a yellow Humvee in a horrible chord. The store had been blown open. Rolling soda cans fanned across the street spraying plumes of foam. Streamers of wood glittered down, a metal pedal rang on the ground, a burning squeegee meteored into a trash can. Everything below us was blanketed in writhing fire. Only one car moved through the wave of hot greasy chemical smoke, before its tires collapsed. An engine popped, a car alarm went off, a door slammed. Erica's motorcycle roared down the hill, banked through the inferno and sped away. The grease pit behind a restaurant had been ignited by falling cinders.

Jasper's hand was on my shoulder. "Let's go."

I slumped in the passenger seat, my forehead on the dashboard, night passing by unseen.

"We're here," Jasper said, parking. I looked up expecting to see the police station where we might finally turn ourselves in or perhaps a hospital where Cy might be being treated for burns but saw instead an alien parking lot and a glowing office supply superstore.

"Jasper, no."

"This will only take a minute."

"No."

"You think Cyrus would want us to give up?"

I didn't think. Clanking through the turnstile, we tried to pass as unlikely entrepreneurs on a late-night clerical errand. In the electronics aisle Jasper browsed CD players.

I found myself before a wall of packing supplies, shaking, eyes melting.

"Tape's rolling," said Jasper.

"Let's call hospitals."

"Let's go."

I opened my mouth and the store shook. The CD did not have enough silence. Blue-vested employees turned like compass needles. I was on my knees, Jasper striking me about the head and shoulders with a mailing tube, telling me to get up.

"Hey cuties," a voice said. A smiling woman in a blue vest held up our CD, twirling it between her fingers. I recognized her from the restaurant. And she me. Jane.

Jasper set his skateboard down, and kicked off. At the end of the aisle, the board flipped into his hand. He slipped between the security devices out the front door.

I looked back at Jane. She was still smiling. "Looks like it's just you and me. You know we don't play industrial in here, it's strictly bland jazz. Orders from above. You look like you're having a rough night. Did somebody die?"

She let me sob in the office. Her manager pulled her aside and they exchanged whispers but nobody asked me any questions or mentioned the CD. When her shift ended, in a car with no muffler she drove me to her apartment. She unlocked several locks and pushed a door into a squalid cauldron of humid laundry. She scooped up a squalling infant. An unsmiling man in stubble seated at a table before a collection of empties took the opportunity to depart, his sharp eyes peeling me. She swept his beer cans into a receptacle and did not bother to say goodbye. "My sister is sick," she said. On an overstuffed chair an incapacitated woman mummified in shawls seemed to confirm this. Jane hovered over her, right hand feeling her brow, left hand picking from the endtable the mutilated kleenex and torn packaging from medicines. "You're still hot. Janis been fed yet?" she asked, taking no for an answer. I sat silently at the table. She rescued a baby bottle from the stove, washed some dishes, cooked salmon steaks.

"Where do you work?" she asked. The cat jumped on the counter and sniffed at the salmon, extending an inquisitive paw.

"SR, I think we're called." She tossed the cat across the kitchen.

"Is that good money?" She dumped a can of cat food into a plastic bowl.

"It has benefits." She poured us each a coffee cup of white wine. Mine was gone before she set my plate down. I ate dinner while she fed the baby in her lap.

"I have two jobs. I'm an art model."

"Ever steal from work?"

"Well, no, not really. It's hard to steal when you're a nude model. Everyone's looking at you, and there's no place to hide anything."

"Where else have you worked?"

"As an art teacher."

"Ever steal anything from school?"

"I was teaching in Brooklyn. It was difficult. There were no tables, they had to work on the floor. There was a closet full of art supplies, an odd selection, never any red. I would collect cardboard boxes so the kids could paint on cardboard, since we were short on paper. And the kids were, you know, kind of difficult, especially thirty at a time. I spent more time dealing with discipline problems than I did teaching painting. I wasn't really paid. On my last day I discovered in the very back of the closet — did you ever see those Dick and Jane readers? I grew up with them, that's how I learned to read. I took it. Oh they were never going to use it. I swear, it was just sitting in the back of a closet. It's a collector's item."

"What's your technique for stealing office supplies?"

"Technique? I'm fat. I can stuff all kinds of things in my clothes. Nobody looks at me."

She held my gaze.

"Do you have more wine?" I asked forwardly.

She refilled my cup. "Are you one of the planners of Steal Stuff From Work Day?"

"I am."

"I've seen the website."

"I wrote that."

"It's inspiring. Most of it. Some of it is stupid. A lot of my friends are making plans for Steal Stuff From Work Day. I'd like to help. Maybe I can donate a shopping cart of office supplies."

She poured more. I tried to make mine last two gulps. I may have told her everything. She said we would call the hospitals in the morning. She let me sleep in her bed; she slept on the couch. Before dawn I left with the rest of the wine. In the darkness it seemed as though she watched me go but neither of us said anything.

How will it end? Dry heat, every haunted object blackening, spewing twisting apparitions. Someone left the pan on the stove too long. On the street a family is trying to drag a smoldering couch to safety. The skies are static, smoke is pouring out of parking meters, newspaper machines combust, a bank is a blaze too bright to look at. A procession of monks with stacks of books balanced on their heads push bicycles through the market past a table where a large, glistening fish writhes. It has swallowed the fisherman. The fish flops and you hear the fisherman's muffled shouting. You have a matchbook. You pin the fish to the table and try to burn a hole in its scales to let the man out. The monks have pushed their bicycles onto a ferry piloted by shipbuilders and are drifting away. Standing on deck with plaintive gestures they implore you to jump into the water, to swim, to join them. Every artifact is bursting into flame, releasing its compacted trauma in ashy billows.

I walked still-dark streets where workers awaiting buses on curbs nodded to me as I passed. I followed a dry concrete canal for a block, crossed it atop a wide pipe and went into the bottom of a parking garage where a single employee sat behind the counter of a not-yet-open rental car office. I knocked on the glass and he left his stool and came to unlock the door.

"Hello," I nodded, "I'm with the club."

He cocked his head.

"SSFW."

He looked me over, told me to wait and went back inside. When he returned he held a set of keys. "Take the jeep. Bring it back by ten tonight with a full tank. Okay?"

"I can do that."

"One week left," he said. "Take good care of the jeep, that one's mine." He locked the door and went back to his computer.

In the colorless, tenuous sunrise I drove through cedar needles up the gravel road. When I came around the final curve, I thought I was at the wrong farm. There was a new building. A horse grazed in a fenced plot, a goat knelt on the grass near the stump it was tied to. The house had been repainted, its shutter fixed. I recognized the red city bus that stood half in the barn. Extra furniture was stacked against the wall. Leaning over a pump was Tom from the bookstore. I parked and walked over to him. Pipes whistled glissandos and water surged into his pail.

"Hey boss. So you know my friends?"

"Intimately. I've even milked their goat."

"Looks like they've been fixing the place up."

"You should stake out a bed. You could have your own room. For awhile."

"Have you seen Jasper? Or Erica?"

"No, but nobody's up yet. They might be here. Go inside and take a look around."

"We had an accident last night. I think somebody might have been hurt. I think we might be in trouble."

Tom looked around but saw no sign of trouble. "Who was hurt?"

"Cyrus?"

He shrugged. "Breakfast in an hour. After that, your choice of digging ditches or harvesting."

I followed him through a screened porch and into the farmhouse. Barb prepared coffee in the kitchen. I wandered through the brand-new furniture in the empty house, inspecting sleeping bodies, but saw nobody I knew. Upstairs I stood in a small library. Every wall was covered with books I recognized.

The peaceful ocean boiled up the coast, mountainsides churning steam. Above the snow-crested volcano, the sun's white circle was eroded by opaque scraps of thicker cloud. A fog-smeared pine-serrated ridgetop. A sense I could melt back into the soggy conifers and rocks. Grey rainbows, temperate winter soup. Cool, pure Pacific air rinsed peeling, arching madronas, erupting poplars, yellow willows, cedar sprigs. A narrow tree grew out of a wide stump, ferns grew out of the narrow tree. Other trees mummified in moss, shaggy chartreuse monsters, a code of mottled birch. Scallops of lichen climbed trunks curving in every direction, frosted with lime.

Evening's grey density infused the overcast sky. An octopusesque pump raised subterranean water and branched into irrigation networks. A cool, steady wind brought the whirr and chirp of birds. Giant pines riffled above the fields of vegetables. Later there came occasional gunfire from the practice range, including, I noted with alarm, the sound of an automatic weapon.

The dilapidated barn was crowned with a spire of some sort, a radio antenna. Behind it was a row of beaten trucks, a repainted Lexus. In the barn wavering fluorescent tubes illuminated walls shelving cans of lacquer, greaser, primer, filler, wash, wax, cleaner, trays of socket wrenches, roof cement. One focus of the space was held by the weight of a sawdusted tablesaw. Coils of chain, rope, hose, wire, rubber hung from boards above. Handles of differently shaped saws corresponded on a hook in the wall. Rows of clipboards hung rank and file from bent nails.

I unstacked interlocking trays of tomatoes, a few of which had been savaged by mice, and carried them out of the barn to the back of the large truck inside of which Ella restacked the boxes of zebras, cosmonauts and other large and grotesquely shaped heirlooms. Food to be taken to friends. Zucchini, onion, garlic. When nobody was looking, I loaded a plastic bag with a swift but discriminate selection of excellent specimens. I went out the side door and put my bag in my jeep.

I believed they would have given them to me if I had asked, but stealing was easier. Inside the new building, Tom stood at an ad hoc desk, face lit by the screen of an older computer. I wanted out.

For my interview, I was taken to a small conference room on the thirtieth floor of a corporate tower filled with a table so long it extended through double doors onto a small balcony that was just a ledge with no railing. There I was seated with a drop just inches behind the wheels of my chair. Wind whipped my tie across my face and tore copies of my résumé from my hands. Hands on thick folders, the search committee stared at me and waited for me to speak. I started, somewhat apologetically, to explain my desire to upgrade my knowledge base. One of them held up a photograph of a stapler. I tried to respond. Another held up a photo of a wheelbarrow. Another held up a photo of a childhood teddy bear. They showed me photos of everything I could remember stealing and things I couldn't. I had nothing to say. They showed me an alarming photograph of a bloody surgical procedure that may have been a circumcision. I stood up, my chair rolled off the edge, the doors blew shut, leaving me with a terrifying fall to the street behind me and locked doors in front of me.

Writing at work is heuristic, dynamic. The trick is to retain a mental focus through constantly interrupted physical activity. Devise and execute multiple simultaneous methods. Send yourself email, upload drafts from work and download them at home, blog. Write at meetings, during breaks, on the bus, in the bathroom stall, at your desk, in elevators, on the second page of a notepad and glance at it occasionally. Write blind: open a word processor in a small window and set the text color to white or the font size too small to read. Write in code, masking poetry as clerical trivia. Remove all the vowels, the string of consonants intelligible to you but ambiguous to anybody else. Cultivate illegibility. Go next door, to other people's place of work, and write in their lobby. Leave yourself voicemail, message yourself, take asynchronous dictation. Train yourself to memorize sentences until you are able to write them down. Discipline yourself to be scatterbrained, never to give unpartitioned cognition to the task at hand. Attack the mountain not by marching toward it across the open slopes, but from behind, treacherously by switchback. Disassemble yourself into a decentralized committee. Any one of you might be blocked, but every one of you cannot be tracked. Communicating through your own mind, you cannot be monitored.

My new job was the sort of workplace where unused computer equipment would collect on every shelf. A laptop had been ordered for me and, through a dealer special nobody had anticipated, a free inkjet printer had been included. The printer sat unopened on a shelf for weeks before I could no longer resist. A coworker had not wanted the speakers for his computer. They sat in a filing cabinet drawer for awhile, then went home with me. If there was a security camera pointed at my cubicle and resources to monitor it, they still would not have detected me taking home discs containing software, fonts and potentially useful files from the computer. A friend of Jasper said he wanted copies of the viruses the lab was studying. I thought he was joking, but gave him copies of everything I could find.

At home, I cleared the empty bottles off the kitchen table. I opened it. It lit up. A white work laptop. A maze of sophisticated circuitry, full of my words for the web. I was a writer now.

While, across town, Jane slept, I uploaded dreams.

Jane and I posed as Hunter's assistant tango instructors to help him steal the sound system. I watched from a folding chair all these battered dancers who had come to lean together and reclaim something elegant. To my surprise and unease, Hunter had me step in when there was a surfeit of men. Jane showed me the step. Out of my ashes something rose. After class, we took down the speakers, and Hunter left with them. Then Jane and I danced again. The terrible despair burned through me, fusing into diamond the dirty coal I carried. There comes a moment without language, musculatures locked in unison movement: we disappear into the music, passing into one another to meet somewhere in the middle. The world went dark outside the empty ballroom. And then it happened. Which was perfect, right then. And of course the trouble with it having been perfect meant that nothing could ever be perfect again, which was also sad. A first and last time, which is all anything ever was — a last first time.

At this point in the story, Cyrus would have turned to me and said a word he carries around. *Fucked* her? You don't understand. I already had her with the music.

***Jane is taking me to her favorite restaurant.** I chase her along the beach. A man hunched over a crank in the sand is struggling to get the waves unstuck. Seagulls pick his wallet to pieces. Inside a red tent we change into bathing suits. We swim far into the ocean, climb marble steps leading out of the warm saltwater. Inside the restaurant are colorful flowers and people eating and we sit down at a table. Somebody gestures to me from the kitchen and it is Jane again. "We haven't cooked yet." Sharing a kitchen with other diners in bathing suits and towels, we cook carrots in wine. We take the kettle up to her room and eat in bed with chopsticks, talking softly because two women are sleeping.*

In the middle of the night I awaken and hear whispering in the bricks. I follow the voices down narrow steps meant for me. Night delivery: there is a cooler of very fresh offal. When I open the lid I see my heart, handfuls of tissue, ice. Jane.

"We still don't know what happened to Cyrus. He's in jail, hospitalized or dead. Beyond our grief at the loss of such a provocative member of the club, he had our treasury in his possession prior to his disappearance. We don't know whether he was caught or what he told to whom. On the positive side, the operations he set up are going smoothly. Every day, hundreds of Starbucks employees take money from the till at the rate of about five dollars per employee per hour. There are manuals to instruct you in techniques of stealing and to identify corporate spies.

"Embezzled funds are used for life support. We've found pro bono lawyers for employees who got in serious trouble. The St. Louis circle bought a building and provides cooperative housing. A communal kitchen is stocked with stolen food and open to everybody. They have criminal dinners every week. This is a model for what a circle can accomplish. The Austin circle has a motor pool of stolen trucks and company cars. In West Virginia a free hospital is staffed and stocked by doctors and nurses who work for and steal from corporate hospitals. I have reports of clothing drives, even armories.

"We have transportation by train, bus, ferry and airline. At Sea-Tac, at three different airlines, members of the club can fly unofficial standby. We can arrange for food and drinks, room and board and taxi rides in many cities. We can set you up with a new identity complete with driver's license and three references. We more or less control the power grids, phone lines and most civilian telecommunications.

"I won't get into the details, but with the help of network administrators everywhere who hate their jobs, we can break into any computer system. Working together, our collective power to erase debt, criminal records, etcetera, is pretty scary. On Steal Stuff From Work Day, IT professionals will reset passwords on corporate, government and university networks, and call in sick."

Supermarket aisles flicker as I walk down them, trying to find the source of the noise. The store has been looted and abandoned. On endlessly stretching empty shelves I find a solitary can of tomatoes. Inside the can is a muffled scream that goes on. I pick it up, look at all sides of it. What would I see if I opened it and stared into the red clumps within?

I went in to work. There was nobody, only tapping coming from Jay's cubicle.

I sat at my computer and tried to remember my responsibilities. It had been a few days since I had finished the logo. I had removed the test tubes and we had settled on a stylized SR. We weren't sure what the acronym would stand for yet, but had sketched out a number of appropriate solutions. I wondered whether Adam White would appear angry when it came time to fire me. I ran the software that would compile records of who had been looking at the Steal Stuff From Work website I had hidden on the server. Opening my email, I almost dropped my coffee. I had 1919 messages. The mail program churned as it attempted to download all this. I set the coffee down on the desk carefully. The first hundred messages were downloaded and they all had the same subject header: POSTING TO STEALSTUFFFROMWORK.COM. The website had a new online forum, and I was sent an email with the text of every posting. It had attracted a lot more interest than I would have believed.

The first email hurt.

> I got myself in some trouble. The FBI is involved. I don't want to turn myself in. I mean, of course I'd lose my job. I don't see how they could catch me. But it was just stupid, I took something I don't even want. Shit. It was so stupid. The library hosted this traveling exhibit. And I knew how to deactivate the alarm. So I took it just because I figured out how. A Shakespeare book, a 'first folio.' Bound in goatskin. 400 yr old book. What do I do?

The next email was a response:

> Read it.

The statistics software finished organizing the data. The number of hits was astronomical, well beyond what our server would normally attract. I clicked tabs that showed different interpretations of the data. The most popular page was a manifesto I had written. I wondered whether the text was traceable to my computer. The geographic breakdown showed that the site was popular in the U.S., Japan, Canada, England, Australia, France, Italy, Germany, New Zealand and the list went on. Thousands of people a day, overwhelmingly from corporate servers between eight a.m. and five p.m. Monday through Friday. The largest number of visitors had come from — I reached for the coffee but my hand was shaking — fbi.gov. I decided to take down the entire website — manifesto, discussion forum, downloadable pamphlets, flyers, templates and all. How could I not get fired for this? A mistake, I rehearsed, a joke. I was just teaching myself the software, I didn't know that site was online. I opened another window to log in to the server. It rejected my password. I made four more attempts, tremulous fingers stabbing keys with great care, before it cut me off.

"You're in trouble," came a soft voice right behind me.

I swiveled, knocking the coffee cup to the floor.

Jane giggled. "Every time I see you, you look really scared. Is it me?"

"No. But — "

"You told me to visit you at work, remember? Probably not, you drank a lot of my wine that night."

My hand flailed an exasperated gesture and she grabbed it and for a moment seemed angry.

"Yes. You're in big trouble. People don't walk out on me. I'm not that bad. You owe me two bottles of wine and a morning."

"Right. Let's get drunk. It's almost eight."

I tried to shut down my computer but it had frozen. I yanked the plug and we threaded our way out of the labyrinth of cubicles where only Jay could be heard.

I bought us a paper bag, bottle and corkscrew, and we walked to the park. At a chess table Jane brought out a stack of business-reply mail envelopes preaddressed to credit unions, magazines, insurance companies. "Here's how we can get the word to mailroom grunts." I had a stack of our cards. We drank wine, stuffed envelopes, dropped the bottle in the trash and the bundle in a mailbox. "Feel better?" she asked. She took me on a tour of the city, stapling flyers to telephone poles outside cafes, record stores, outfitters and jewelers, any place we would have shopped. We stopped at a bar to have martinis and to post notices in red marker in bathroom stalls. In the suffocating vapor of a laundromat, Jane interviewed a weary attendant in a pressed uniform. At a factory parking lot, she talked a security guard into letting us put cards beneath employee windshield wipers. Moving through a dystopian indoor mall, she asked me, "Want to shoplift?" "We aren't thieves," I reminded her. Behind the counter of a pizzeria a young woman read the card out loud uncertainly. "Don't steal from your customer. Don't steal from your coworker. Steal from your boss. stealstufffromwork.com." She popped her gum. "Hey papa!" An immense man with white chef's hat and flour-white beard appeared from the kitchen carrying a rolling pin. His thick fingers held the card up to where he could squint at it.

"What is this here?"

"Are you the owner of the restaurant?"

"This is my business. This is my family. What is this here?"

"A mistake," Jane smiled, and bowed toward the exit, pulling me out of the violent hail of bilingual invective. She turned the city inside out, routing unseen streetsweepers, bicycle messengers, utility workers climbing poles or crawling beneath the sidewalk, mechanics under taxis, uniformed fast-food workers cleaning grease traps, attendants in underground parking garages where slammed car doors reverberated through colorless cement labyrinths, Hispanic maids pushing carts of soap through threadbare hotel basements. Beneath a shining marquee, a blue-vested cashier in a glass booth stared out with an inscrutable expression after Jane slid our card into the metal trough. The secretary of a dental office responded to our card with shock. Unwilling to discuss the matter, she sought to usher us out of the building. We presumed she had operations in progress. Jane shone on, drawing me into new neighborhoods perpendicular to any beaten path. We ran to catch a bus and sat in the back. She took my hand and traced a line on my palm. "You have a broken life line. See. . . there's a gap. It ends here, and starts again here. It jumps."

"Do you believe that?"

"Do you?"

"I believe we're all going to die."

"Okay." She smiled out the window at the boarded up storefronts scrolling by but kept my hand in her lap. I hoped the bus would drive on to Mexico. She met me at work. Did she steal me?

She remembered something:

"Guess what?"

"What?"

"Yesterday I saw Jasper get into an army jeep."

"Was he arrested?"

"No. He got in. He was picked up."

"Where did you see this?"

"By the Hendrix museum."

"Were you with him?"

"I was following him."

"Why?"

"He likes to fuck and run. Me, I prefer a little affection. In lieu of cuddling I thought I'd see what was more important than me."

"You mean you guys are. . . dating?"

"Not exactly. He hasn't asked me on a date yet."

"I had no idea. I thought — I didn't know you were with him."

"Well he's with some soldiers."

As I stood to signal a stop outside my office, I saw men in suits I did not like the look of walking into our building with Adam White, who was supposed to be out of town. I sat back down and kept on riding.

Finally, Jane got off. I got off.

I bought a newspaper, circled some ads.

I got back on. Later, I got off at home, got my toothbrush and some clothes. Then I rode the wrong way, from home to the end of the line.

When the customers are done eating, they push away their plates, get up and leave without paying or tipping. I tell the manager, he shrugs. Everything is free now, he explains. A pang of confusion hits me: then what am I doing working here? I take the next order to the kitchen. The cooks look so pissed it hurts. I gently clip my ticket to the wheel, gingerly spin it, and tiptoe away. The dishwasher has left and dishes are piling up. Trying to help, I load a rack of plates and run it through the machine, getting mostaccioli on my sleeve. Back in the dining room, new customers stand around by the front door, waiting to be seated. The manager is nowhere to be seen. I seat them and tell them I will be right with them. On my way to get water glasses, fingers snap at me from a booth. It is the manager, he has seated himself and he asks for a bone-dry double martini with three olives. "Who gets to be customer?" I ask. He glares at me.

Lightning but no rain. I needed a place to sleep. I tried to remember whether Jasper still worked at the bookstore. I had kept my key. Erica had been moonlighting other high-altitude jobs. She was a window washer downtown, and she had a job changing bulbs on the Space Needle. She had agreed to meet me there at night when it was closed to the public. It was the gaudy hood ornament of a car that had never been built. "Hard times, kid," she punched my arm, she punched elevator buttons. The city slid down around us. The water was deep and wide. I saw the lit decks of ships and wondered whether there were captains aboard. We came out onto a maintenance level, a catwalk encircling the legs, metal floating above a circus of city light. A north wind hit us. "You want out, you're afraid. Your world is crumbling. It should be. Now you're going to watch me do my job. See that bulb burned out on the right?"

"I'll wait right here, thanks. Hey. I think I see a fire burning downtown."

"You might," she sang into the wind. Her safety line banged against the metal as she descended. A fog had started to obscure the traffic below us, which was fine with me. I clung to the cold metal rail and blinked tears out of my eyes. A new bulb came on below me. "Is that a fire on. . . Mt. Ranier?"

"Could be an airplane. You need a place to sleep?"

"Looks that way."

"You can sleep here."

"No, I don't think I could." My eyes were shut. The wind was arctic. Erica's boot-heels reverberated through the catwalk as she walked back over to where I had braced myself. "This'll be the place to be tomorrow night for Steal Stuff From Work Day," she said, "view of everything. Of course we'll be in control of the elevator. Come on up. Bring champagne."

"I think I'm going to find Jasper and sleep at the bookstore. But who knows where Jasper is?"

The question hung there. I saw what looked like another fire, this one near the docks.

"He might be sleeping with Jane out at the farm."

I said nothing. If I jumped, for how many seconds would I fly?

"That boy knows too many weird crazies."

"Tell me about it," I said.

"I'd sleep with you," she said. "You snore?"

I hadn't considered that. "Let's go to the bookstore," I said.

"You sure?"

"No. I don't know. I'm worried."

"No you aren't. Ever ridden a motorcycle before?"

Her flannel whipped my cheeks as she sped me past the port. The wind stripped my body of sensation. What she said had opened wounds. But I still had the night to contend with. Zipping past the downtown, I hung to her, frozen to her back. The road up to the farm was lined with parked cars. The barnraising was in progress. The field was covered with tents, buses, and an ambulance and someone was being amplified. Two kids stood drinking well water out of plastic cups by torchlight. "Hey," I asked them, "what's with the police cars? Is there a raid?"

They were dressed as valets. I realized they had just gotten off work. Perhaps they had driven here in requisitioned luxury cars. "No raid, man. Those cars are ours."

The cheering was drowned out by a helicopter landing. It was emblazoned with the insignia of a local news show and lit up the grass. The propwash extinguished a campfire and sent an unstaked tent tumbling. A young man ran away from the wind-flattened circle holding his hat to his head. An ice cream truck trundled toward the helicopter as a news crew emerged with camera equipment and ran, hunching beneath the rotor, to the truck and were given popsicles. Behind us a bulldozer came up the farm road. A descending whine as power to the prop was cut and people started to move closer to the helicopter. Erica put her finger through my beltloop and pulled me back to the bike. I climbed on behind her, and she took us back to Seattle.

"Jasper?" The bookstore returned no echo. The door clinked shut behind Erica and me. I reached for the light switch, but instead of buzzing fixtures came a flash and pop, then lights moving back and forth upstairs. We climbed the steps into the cookbook room. Through the doorway, a wall of flames ate through history. Plumes everywhere ignited books. I pushed over a burning shelf of economics texts to try stamping them out but the shelf was instead filled with romance novels that smelled of kerosene. They were soggy, and stamping them into mush made them burn faster. The fire passed from book to book, greedily ingesting pages in no particular order, leaving moldier volumes untouched, vaulting from shelf to shelf without regard for category. Perhaps poetry might be spared. But we would have to get hoses in here and spray water around. Had our absentee employer thought to provide a chemical extinguisher for our safety? Was that aspect of my training neglected? I looked closer at poetry and saw a book called *Dress for Success,* wet with solvent. "Is there another way out of here?" asked Erica. Some of the shelves were bare. A wave of smoke bent me over coughing. I pointed back the way we had come in. Erica shook her head. A shelf of oversized art books collapsed across the hall leading to the fire escape in a gust of sparks. I turned into the former elevator shaft where science fiction overstock was kept. I pointed to several buckets on the floor. "It leaks when it rains," I shouted. "The sky must be above." Erica pushed the ceiling panels up into the shaft and jumped onto a shelf. Kicking L. Ron Hubbard paperbacks aside, she put her shoulders into the hole. I watched cowboy boots scrabble against the wall until one found a rivet and she was gone. A tattooed hand came down for me, I grabbed her wrist and she pulled me up into an airy elevator shaft. A service ladder was mounted to the wall. We climbed toward the night, into an old elevator shed hung with large pulleys. A grid gave way to Erica's boot and we passed through into the cooler roof air.

Over a low wall and down a few feet we crossed another roof. It wasn't clear whether the fire would spread to this building. I walked around the edge and found only a smooth drop on all sides. Erica paused before a locked shed. Sirens rose. She tried a few keys from her ring, and then her boot-heel. The door bounced open, scraping roofgravel. We followed a metal handrail down three flights of dark concrete steps, through a door into a narrow space lit in a flickering wash of light and amplified voices. Peeking around a corner we found we were behind a movie screen. It was almost dawn — this wasn't a scheduled screening.

We moved forward to the front row where, in the intermittent light that streamed from a projectorbulb, we saw a sparse gallery of people engaged in an illicit after-hours showing hosted by an off-duty projectionist. In the front row was Jasper, eating popcorn. He was bald again. I walked over and stood in front of him.

"The bookstore is burning," I said.

He spat a kernel at my feet.

"Don't be sentimental," he said.

There was a commotion and a handful of firemen burst in beneath the exit light, looking about confusedly. Seeing no fire in this space, they paused to watch the film.

The coffee is now the customer's property. *The cup is still the owner's property. The server's grace is available for an optional coin. The soil is the plantation owner's property. The electricity will always be the power company's property. The profits are the owner's. The work is not the worker's.*

The coffee cup, beans, sugar, milk, napkin and water were manufactured, harvested, milked, roasted, refined, pasteurized, packaged, loaded, shipped, unloaded, unpackaged, purified, piped, prepared.

On their labels and lists of ingredients, no mention is made of people.

Correction: only the strained beans are the customer's property. The water still belongs to the sky.

In the Port of Tacoma titanic white camels, in the Port of Seattle gargantuan orange giraffes, bellies hung with parabolic cable entrails, graze at the foaming ocean. Standing over giant ships stacked with colored blocks, these massive cranes could dismantle skyscrapers. We will ride them across the water to where the skyline poses like a family portrait with a toy top.

It seemed like it might rain. A lone gull stitched the sky, winging over this fringe of civilization. Through a smoldering chink in the cloud the sun appeared briefly over the sea. The tops of radio towers turned pink, scored with shadows of rivets. A disintegrating structure of crumbling wooden piles sagged into the sea, a stubble of black stumps where a pier once stood. Oil drums floated in the glittering sound. On deck a solitary seaman moved a clanking ladder among pipes and coils. A distant sailboat looked like a linen napkin in a mudpuddle. This was the day?

Leaves and wrappers driven by wind skittered through broken streets. Jasper kicked his skateboard through desolation. There weren't many people on the street but they were his. A phalanx of hooded fellow skateboarders rolling in formation nodded to him. A cab seemed to flicker its lights. On my bicycle, I coasted behind him.

A hum lay over things, emanating from a brick monolith impaled by three smokestacks on the crumbling shoreline. *Puget Hydroelectric Substation* was etched into the building. How many millions of bricks in it? Ancient and with no sign of life behind its twenty-foot arched red-framed windows. How many hundreds of panes of glass? Beside it a looming junglegym of high-voltage transformers articulated a matrix out of air. Iron towers held aloft cables pointing in every direction across the sky. Red moss climbed a wall hung with a maze of pipes and valves. Ferns wove through a chain-link fence topped with sagging barbed wire. Piles of gravel, heaps of sand lay about its empty parking lot. I pedaled between unmanned security gates up into the complex. Hissing boilers were fed by green pipes emerging from underground. Stray cables coiled about a smashed hubcap. An American flag flapped gaily over all this.

In the shadow of a recessed doorway came an eruption of a match, its flare revealing Jasper's face before it was sucked into the red prick of a handtwisted cigarette. He threw the match down and his eyes spoke.

I followed his shining head down corrugated metal steps. A wet smell, a rushing noise. I pushed through a scraping metal door onto a catwalk where caged blue bulbs shone over a sluiceway. Our steps rang from concrete walls ornamented with dials and gauges.

I sat in a long narrow locker room. The flickering overhead spasmed with a tortured buzz. Plaster shards from punctured sheetrock had left white splashes on the cracked cement floor. Cobweb-shrouded fluorescent tubes hung beneath a maze of loose wires and pipes wrapped in gauze, marked with chartreuse splotches of corrosion. Wooden steps led up to a brown door whose glass panes had been replaced by plywood. Ribbed cables sprouted from a fusebox. A humming vending machine in need of restocking, having only a single candybar, cast a yellow glow over the enamel table where I sat beside the fluted aluminum ashtray. A wallmounted timeclock marked every minute with a clunk. Jasper sat on an overturned bucket in the corner staring at the ground. "This is the real insomniac club."

The squeak of blade on stone. I jerked. A hunched and wizened man in overalls and Sonics cap with a garbagecan on wheels stood in the doorway and took me in. The overhead went off. When it came on he was sitting at the table across from me, lit cigarette between two trembling fingers, sneakered toe quivering nervously. Unblinking eyes sat back in his head and sized me up, eyebrows raised matter-of-factly. He didn't look happy. Grey hair shaved close to his thin neck, salt-and-pepper moustache hung above an ajar frown. Skin wrinkled like canyon stone, concentric ripples beneath the eyes, furrows radiating a map of anxieties, a record of his every wince. He was missing teeth and spoke a slackjawed, halting, aspirant tremolo, words arriving regularly as out of a teletype.

"Jasper has told me about your Steal Stuff From Work Day."

"Ah."

"Why a day?"

"So it hurts."

"So after 2000 years it hurts for one day. You are the mosquito who needs to become the dagger. This is no holiday. Tomorrow there will be no power. Nothing will move in Seattle. The tension of accumulated pain can only be released quickly like a bear trap, not slowly like a windup watch. In the next world, the dull sheen of the product will be replaced by the glow of art. Objects will be brought back to life. They will no longer be mute, they will speak of the intelligences that touched them."

He poured us each a glass of water.

"Are you ready for the real work? The work you give to?"

I look into the janitor's eyes. Blue irises, circumference of white, look at me. I am unshaven, my eyes burnt, but my shirt is as white as clouds. I try to speak, but the control tower is radioing me not to take off. "This bird belongs to the one who flies it," you say. You roll the kegs, one by one, out the back door; they clunk heavily down steps and grind into the gravel alleyway where somebody pounds a railroad spike into one of them and a geyser of beer rains over the people holding cups to the sky. You slide the entire drawer out of the cash register, zip it into your backpack and walk out, leaving a sign on the door saying FREE GIVEAWAY. You push the carrel of books out onto the loading dock and tip it into the trunk of your car. You unplug the Wacom tablet, the portable hard drive, the speakers, the scanner, the flat monitor, and stow it all in a large duffel bag, turning off lights on a machine stripped of all interface. Punching out with a pocket full of pharmaceutical-grade morphine. You unscrew the four corners of the bathroom mirror, remove it, then unscrew the security camera behind it. Your jumpsuit has many pockets. In your rear-view mirror you see the astonished supervisor arrive onto the loading dock as you bounce away with the full truck of phonebooks. Vegetables for everybody. Infrared sights for the children, twine and bayonets to mark the perimeters of your herb garden. Babysitting is much easier with date rape drugs; junior is comatose and you have found the jewelry. Mr. White stands agape, nine iron in his hand, as you drive his golf cart over the edge of the course and into traffic. In the evidence room, shelves of bagged, labeled drugs. It only takes a minute to upload your boss's personal email to the web. You drive right on by the bus stop and the people watch you pass. You rev the purring Jaguar and in a cloud of rubber smoke and go out through the showroom window. Most of the guns go in the duffel bag, but the antique silver pistol that killed the bear goes in your belt. A lethal virus in a vial in your pocket. Disconnecting the alarms was easy; the tricky part will be trying to fit the Picassos in your van. You set all the birds and animals free.

The customer cracks open the wallet. In an eruption of escaping cash, fluttering bills pour into the rafters. Across the city cash registers explode from the pressure. Banks are craters, the bodies of rich people are discovered miles from their homes. In the hearts of large cities, cyclones form. Earthquakes rock the Swiss Alps and California. Money tumbles southward through the atmosphere, blanketing deserts in green.

He wrote: you can't build a tower that high and put all your resources into the top. The men who rule the world would not know how to use a gun, but make no mistake: they rule by violence. Maybe it will take an earthquake to fell the tower. Or maybe we will pull it down. Either way it cannot stand.

He has accidentally flushed the last sponge down the toilet he was scrubbing. On his knees, staring at his reflection in the bowl while the hissing tank refills, he is crushed by accumulated gravity. This rippling mirror is a holographic fragment in which he glimpses the compressed futility of his life. As the sibilance subsides he becomes aware of, from behind the wall, a faint thumping and laughing.

Ever since Steal Stuff From Work Day, the television had been broadcasting disaster. Some stations were off the air, having had key equipment stolen. Some seemed to be on the wrong channels. It was like being in a different city. An outbreak of a new disease dropped to the number two story but the two items became confused. The rains added to the confusion, flooding low-lying neighborhoods. An explosion in a hydroelectric substation on the shoreline had caused power surges that sparked fires across the grid. Sea water had breached the Seattle subterrain, flooding basements, sewer mains and underground tunnels. To keep public order, army troops arrived from Fort Lewis, outside Tacoma. A chain reaction of outages that swept most of the U.S. and Toronto was suspected to be caused by employees of power facilities, though investigation had so far revealed only outdated equipment. Even now most of North and South America were suffering rolling blackouts. Las Vegas had, inexplicably, been evacuated. Wealthy Seattleites barricaded themselves at home in fright and a few departed the city on extended vacations. Guards barricaded gated communities, trapping employers and police in their neighborhoods. In other cases, they locked people out of their neighborhoods while cleaning ladies distributed copied housekeys and entrance codes. Wrong prescriptions put night watchmen to sleep and gave CEOs hallucinations and diarrhea. An invisible army of the ordinary destroyed, disabled and discombobulated, spreading fear without frightening. A human heart was stolen from Seattle General, reported the Real News Network. That disgusted him, but he suspected that

Cy would have appreciated it. Maybe Cy did it. The story was uncorroborated and was not repeated but served to intensify the panic. A former priest had somehow stolen a churchbell. A passenger jetplane hijacked by its own flight crew was forced down by the military, crashlanding in a mall in Kansas City. "It is no exaggeration to say that the barometer of American life has changed overnight." The television stood in a corner of the empty lobby depicting a nation in apparent chaos. "So solidly did 65,000 organized workers steal from work that 40,000 other employees were also idled by lack of transport and work. Strikers served food, supplied hospitals and kept peace in the streets with astonishing organization and efficiency," the newspaper, conversely, reported. But RNN had not picked up the story about the peace in the streets.

For these things speak
Of a NEW POWER.
And a NEW WORLD
That they do not feel
At HOME in.

There had been no guests all night. Traffic had slowed to a whisper outside and a distant clock tower rang three. Cleaning completed, slumped at the front desk, Kemp would stare at these scenes of flames and bodies and white suited epidemiologists entering quiet buildings and not hear what was said. At one point he noticed to his surprise a glint beside the eye of an otherwise unaffected and impeccably preened newscaster. It cut to an interstitial; the news program was called "The World: What You Make It." Bored, he broke into the bed-and-breakfast's office using a credit card a guest had left behind. He had no plans to steal anything, he was just curious. There was little of value inside, but now unfolded before him was a blueprint of the building. On the third floor of this renovated mansion there were two guest rooms, but the floorplan showed three, as well as a nonexistent narrow stairway leading up from behind the small kitchen that was now used only for special events. A serious doctor working a disaster on a street at night had pulled his breathing mask down to say something to the camera, and he spoke for quite some time. Behind him was some frantic activity and the pulse of ambulance lights.

Kemp snapped a lightswitch and panels blinked on above the small kitchen. There had been a wedding party that day and the normally bare counters were strewn with the celebration's remains, including a case of red wine. He pulled a bottle from the box and held it up for inspection. "Randall Harris Merlot ought-three, interesting choice." He decanted a paper cup of the red, cut himself a piece of cake, and smoothed the blueprint on a steel counter, comparing the room to its design. The kitchen seemed smaller than its outline as depicted in the floor plan. Against the back wall where the staircase was drawn was a row of tall cupboards. He popped the doors, all eight of them. Shelves of plates, glasses, saucers, towels, bottles of shampoo, ashtrays, napkins. In the cabinet on the end a broom leaned among a heap of rubber gloves, sponges and solvents. Kemp frowned and leaned forward and put his hand to the panel in the back. He rapped it with his knuckles. When he pushed it, it bent slightly. His eyes examined its perimeter in the shadow. Near the top was a short horizontal section of rope. He stepped inside and put his hand through the loop of rope and pulled. Pushed. Lifted. The back of the cabinet, a large piece of plywood, popped free.

In the office drawer, a flashlight and a ring of assorted keys. A buzzing from the front. Behind the desk he looked into the small monitor. The outdoor security camera's black-and-white image with rolling timestamp depicted from above two officers of the law standing outside the door apparently requesting admission. He paused.

When the old woman arrived the next morning, she found the front desk unattended. A few anxious members of the wedding party were eager to check out and put the excesses of the event behind them. She moved slowly into the kitchen, was not sure where their wine went, thanked them for the dubious gift of whatever cake might be left over, was not sure where her clerk went, but presumed correctly he would not be back, resolving to balance the accounts to see whether he had taken cash from the drawer. As her memory was shaky, she went to type a statement for the police but couldn't find her manual typewriter. Later that morning police arrived and were asking questions about one of her employees, but she did not know where he was. She showed them the address he used on his application and paperwork and they left.

A dank light oozed through a grimy window into the musty attic room that—according to the blueprint—had originally been the mansion's servants' quarters. Later it had been a cramped effort at a single room, and then the door was walled over and, judging from the fixtures, the space had apparently been used as some sort of illicit indoor garden. The sink still worked though the toilet would not flush. There was no bed, only a chair and a wooden pallet as furnishings. With the extra pillows and blankets he had taken from the linen room it was a serviceable squat. Halfway through the first bottle of wine he threw himself at the window and struggled to open it, but it was sealed in place by the warping of wood.

At the base of the unused servant's stairs, the hidden space behind the kitchen cabinets offered storage for broken furniture accessed by a seldom-used back door that had once been a servant's entrance.

In the parking lot a sodium arc light overlooked shining parked cars. A doorway scraped open yielding a grimy former hotel employee holding the neck of an almost-empty bottle of wine. He leaned in the shadows and the night breathed around. A flicker showing nobody else was accompanied by a prolonged crashing of thunder. A patter of drops seemed to ensure his solitude. He moved out unsteadily. The bottle crashed in a dumpster and another rumble rippled through the sky. A siren wailed.

Through an unmarked door on a windowless building with no sign he stepped into a crowd of shouting drinkers. Pink and blue lighting apparatuses hung from scaffolding. Giant mirrors, fifteen feet up the wall, overlooked the blue neon bar where bartenders furiously pushed drinks out into a haze lit by a flicker of strobes. There was a single unoccupied red felt pool table.

Pushing his way through a dense field of men to a small table clothed in red plastic, he sat beneath neon shapes and a rotating mirror ball.

Dark corridors I crawl. Knives all around. What will keep me from being thrown from the tower.

He had trouble ordering the drink when the waitress came around. His lips moved but he had no voice.

At the far end of the room a dancer walked onstage and the thudding music started. Jane's body was a money magnet. As she sashayed down the walkway, in the depths of men's jeans wallets forced their way to the surface, sprouting leaves. Petals from their blossoms adhered to her body, tucking themselves into her garters and g-string. Lap dances wrung the last few bills out of their pants like ecstatic butterflies escaping from spent cocoons. The men stood to express enthusiasm. Voluptuous, bored, undulating, she taunted them from the frank armor of her nudity. Kemp looked away whenever she sought his gaze. The last of his money squirmed, trying to escape. His whiskey arrived and he paid for it but did not tip. He felt the room turn against him. The first burning sip brought him to a place of tranquility. The flashing lights and jiggling breasts and thumping beat were things he could understand. The men were taunted and degraded until, drained of cash, they slunk out the door. One of the less servile shouted something that sounded like it ended in "whore" and bouncers materialized at his sides like buff genies to escort him from the premises.

Next act. One birthday boy whose buddies must have proffered a mighty tip was led onto the walkway, where he was lashed to a pole, his hands tied behind him. A trio of topless women forced a hat shaped like the head of a penis onto his head, and shook their breasts in his face. The other men were vocal in their approval of this event. Kemp cracked his mouth but had no voice, the neon turned him into a blinking skeleton. The fetid air seemed moist with germs.

A guy tapped him. Kemp looked up. The guy gestured for Kemp to follow him. Kemp tried to query the guy but nobody heard. The guy took him back into a dressing room, through a hubbub of naked and half-naked women applying makeup, brushing hair, straightening stockings and calling their kids, and up some stairs.

They stepped into a murky room with caramel carpeting. They were behind the one-way mirrors above the bar. Immediately below, fingers tapped out transactions on cash register keys. A posh office lit by a few muted cones stretched back. Behind the desk was Cyrus. He had gained weight, he seemed inflated and pasty. He stood halfway up.

"I thought that was you," he said proudly.

Kemp wasn't sure if he could move.

"I waited tables with him," exclaimed Cy to the guy, who nodded and left. Cy pulled open a drawer, withdrew a crystal decanter and heavy octagonal glasses that made noise when he set them down. He poured them each a generous double. Mouth watering, Kemp picked up his, and the fumes brought him tears.

"Where you working?" Cy asked.

"I'm not."

"I heard you were a hotel desk clerk."

"I quit. I'm still living there though."

"How can you afford it?"

"They don't know I'm there."

Cy seemed impressed with that but had nothing to say. He pulled out a silver cigar case, and they each took one. Cy had to show him how to chop it with the guillotine on his desk.

After the first puff Cy smiled and walked to the window to look down upon the action below. A teenage woman was dancing in a pool of light. A man lay back on the stage with a bill in his teeth and the woman extracted it with her labia to the delight and astonishment of the clientele. Servers crawled across the floor like ants on a carcass. Cash poured into the registers from all corners of the establishment. Bartenders moved from bottle to customer to cash register, pointing at the next to be served. Waitresses returned to the bar with money and went back into the crowd balancing glasses on trays. A torrent of alcohol rinsed away builtup cash.

Cy gestured with his cigar. "Watch that cocktail waitress in the haltertop. See, she's ordered a drink, the bartender is getting it. The bartender didn't ring it up. Okay, now look, she sold it to that guy at table B12. She took the money. I think she's taking about ten dollars an hour that way, methodically, every third customer. The bartender must be in on it. She works so fast she still brings in as much as the others."

"You going to fire her?" I coughed up a small laugh.

"I'll give her a choice."

"Trouble you for more of this. . . brandy?"

"Armagnac. Help yourself. People who don't steal don't work as hard. Anyway, if there's trouble with the books, it's good to know who to blame it on."

"Do you pay the dancers?"

"No. I barely pay the servers."

"Have any trouble with police?"

"Me? Nah. You?"

"I believe I may be wanted."

"Good to be wanted."

"No."

"Well, right now they want everybody."

"How long you owned this place?"

"Not too long."

"How did you pay for it?"

"Pays for itself."

"Ah. We thought you were dead."

"No kidding. People are dying everywhere. It's on the news. Major disease outbreak."

"In America?"

"Right here in fucking Seattle."

The end of the shift. The cashiers pulled rolls of tape and drawers from the register, the next shift slid new ones in. Kemp watched them enter the office one by one and stack the drawers on Cy's desk. Some asked for favors. The one who was stealing expressed his concern about one of the other workers. Cyrus smiled. "Leave me any?" he joked, gesturing at the drawer. The man exited without further comment.

Cy divided the receipts into two piles. "One for me, one for Uncle Sam." Fingers dancing on an adding machine, he accounted for half of the sales, filling a bank deposit envelope with cash. He fed the other pile of register tape into a quietly humming shredder, then sorted the unaccounted for cash into stacks, snapping a rubber band around each one and tucking it into a shoebox beneath his desk.

Ka-ching.

In a corner, the black bear stared at Kemp, it seemed, piteously.

The next day snow fell. Kemp sat up on the pallet, and stared out the tiny window as he lit one of the hand-rolled cigarettes Cyrus had given him.

He began to type.

As the sun went down, blinking red lights played on the window, whether from holiday decorations or emergency he did not know.

thanks to

brian e
cristy s
dirk s
iain m
jeremy c
marty r
natalija g & ognjen r
nick m
paul k
rick b

also

chuck p
friedrich e & karl m
and the dude from fscked.org

Steal Stuff From Work by Jasper Pierce

second hardback Keyhole Edition 2010

paper: isbn-13 978-0-9801392-2-8
isbn 0-9801392-2-8 $11.11

cloth: isbn-13 978-0-9801392-3-5
isbn 0-9801392-3-6 $25.00

Library of Congress Control Number: 2008925637

spinelessbooks.com
stealstufffromwork.com

cover image: *Lawn Darts* by Scott Westgard

SPINELESS BOOKS  URBANA, ILLINOIS

www.ingramcontent.com/pod-product-compliance
Lightning Source LLC
LaVergne TN
LVHW101322110826
845152LV00011B/30
* 9 7 8 0 9 8 0 1 3 9 2 3 5 *